MICHAEL DECAMP

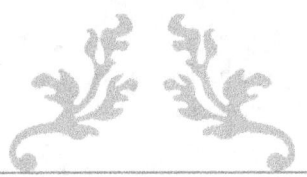

CUTTERS NOTCH INTERLUDES

A Collection of Short Stories

Michael DeCamp

Copyright © 2020 by Michael DeCamp
Published by Jurnee Books, an imprint of Winged Publications

Editor: Cynthia Hickey
Book Design by Winged Publications

All rights reserved. No part of this publication may be reproduced, stored in a retrieval system, or transmitted in any form or by any means—electronic, mechanical, photocopying, recording, or otherwise—without the prior written permission of the publisher. The only exception is brief quotations in printed reviews. Piracy is illegal. Thank you for respecting the hard work of this author.

This book is a work of fiction. Names, characters, Places, incidents, and dialogues are either products of the author's imagination or used fictitiously.

Any resemblance to actual persons, living or dead, or events is coincidental. Scripture quotations from The Authorized (King James) Version.

Fiction and Literature: Inspirational
Thriller Suspense Mystery
Paranormal
Young Adult

All rights reserved.
ISBN: 979-8-3303-6822-8

Table of Contents

Out of the Depths of Abandon	Page 1
Penny's Pet Peeve	Page 36
Linda's Window	Page 41
Davy's Gift	Page 53
Rose and the Wooden Box	Page 68

Dear Readers,

This collection of short stories represents over a decade of fun as I explored this crazy little imaginary town. When I first discovered writing, I realized that if I could imagine it, I could make it happen by writing it down. Further, if I did it well, others could see the events unfold, too. I hope that happens as you read these pages. The world of Cutters Notch, Indiana continues to expand in my head, so I expect there will be more fun and weird stories to come.

I want to take a moment to thank my wife, Nancy DeCamp. You were the first to knock the rough edges off these stories. I also want to thank my editor, Sherri Stewart for doing all the fine tuning. She's the one who made the words pop. Thank you Sarah Joy Freese for being a supportive agent and thank you Cynthia Hickey for believing in my work and giving it a published life.

Finally, I want to thank you, the reader, for indulging my imagination. I truly hope you enjoy the adventures hidden within these pages. Much of what you will find will provide you with insight into some of the people and places you will experience in my upcoming sequel, Nozomi's Battle, and the third novel in the series which is still unnamed and over the horizon.

Good reading,
Mike
June 2020

Out of the Depths of Abandon

If you were like the crow soaring high above the neighboring treetops, Tim and his ten-year-old son, Tony, would look like ants skittering back and forth on the grass. They'd fill the wheelbarrow with weeds, sticks, brush, and soil. Then they'd cart it off to the nearby woods to dump the debris. Slowly, being careful to avoid poison ivy, they cleared out the botanical camouflage that kept the great old slab of limestone hidden from view in the middle of their new home's backyard.

It was an odd hunk of stone sitting all alone in that spot for no apparent reason. Flat on top and almost perfectly round, it appeared to have been fashioned into that shape and then moved to its present location for a reason that was lost on everyone. Even the real estate agent who handled their purchase could find no historical reason for it to be there—no remains of an old grist mill, no antiquated mine. Limestone mines had been common in the area, but it seemed that this stone's location had been established long before the mining had even begun.

Despite its longevity in that spot and since it seemed to lack any historical significance, Tim decided the hunk of rock needed to go. A swimming pool was destined to take its place as the focal point of the property. He had visions of something inground—a nice patio with lounge chairs and umbrellas surrounding a cool pool of water on a hot, sunny day.

It was lunch time when the man and his son finally cleared out the last load and stood side-by-side, shovels in hand, gazing at their handiwork. Sweat streaked the accumulated dust on their faces.

Tim studied the rock for a long time, then, "That is such an odd place for that stone."

"What's so weird about it, Dad?" the boy asked.

"Well," Tim scratched his chin. "It looks like it was moved there on purpose, like someone meant for it to be there, but there's no record of who did it or why it was done. It's almost like it was done prehistorically." He gestured toward the rest of the yard and the nearby forest. "I mean, look. There aren't any other similar stones nearby."

"Do you think maybe the Indians moved it there?" Tony asked.

"Maybe…" Tim trailed off, then said, "It could have been the Adena-Hopewell people, I suppose."

"Who?"

"Do you remember when we went up to Mounds State Park in Anderson and saw the Great Mound?"

"Yeah." Tony grinned. "We hiked the trails along the river and had a great picnic. The playground was cool, too."

"They used to live throughout this area. Just as the reasons why they built that mound are long gone, maybe the same people fashioned and put this rock here—for whatever reason. Some of the mounds are burial sites or were ceremonial places, but nobody knows why they built some of the other mounds. They just disappeared. Nobody knows where they went or what happened to them. It's like they had this great community but then it just vanished."

"That's weird, Dad."

"Yes, it is. Weird is a good word for it."

The back door of the house opened, so they turned to look. There standing by one of the porch's ornate wooden pillars was Tim's beautiful young wife of sixteen years. Even now he couldn't keep his eyes off her. The years hadn't taken away her youthful beauty. In her tan shorts and short-sleeved, red polka-dotted top, Traci still looked like she did the day they met. The shade of the nearby giant sycamore tree cast shifting shadows across her lightly freckled face and auburn ponytail. The whole picture was stunning.

"Lunch is ready," she called. "Wash up and I'll set it up here on the porch."

A few minutes later, they sat at the rectangular glass patio table that fit nicely onto their spacious porch. Tim's fifteen-year-old daughter, Teresa, joined them. She plopped down with her back against the wooden railing that matched the pillars and carefully arranged a notebook and accompanying Bible to the left of her plate.

"Are you going somewhere after lunch?" her mom asked.

"Yeah, the teen group has an afternoon devo today. Jilly is picking me up, and we're all going over to Spring Mill for the day."

Tim smiled. "So, you're making some new friends here in Cutters Notch?"

"Yeah," Teresa replied. "Jilly's fun and her dad's one of the leaders at our new church. We hang out at school some. She's been wanting me to come to youth group. The church seems cool, so why not?"

"Well, I'm glad you're making wise choices." Traci shrugged and looked over at Tim. "And I'm glad you're making some good friends, too."

Tim nodded.

Although Teresa sometimes seemed a little over the top, Tim was proud of her childlike faith, and he wished his matched hers in its unwavering nature.

Turning to Tim, Traci asked, "Is the stone ready to move yet?"

"Yep," he answered. "I'll get Jim Abbott to bring over his tractor tomorrow, and we'll drag it into the woods."

"You can't move it with the truck?" Tony asked.

"Nope. It's way too heavy for the Chevy, but Jim's John Deere will make light work of it."

"Cool," said the boy.

"I don't really like that man," Traci said, referring to Jim Abbott. "He's crude and sorta nasty. The way he stares at me makes me uncomfortable."

"I'll keep an eye on him," Tim assured her. "He's just here to move the stone and then he'll be gone. I promise."

"Okay, then, I guess." Traci was staring at a paper she'd pulled out of a folder that was stuffed with yellowed pages printed with articles and pictures, plus some old newspaper clippings. She pulled a few more out and spread them around her on the table. There was a light breeze, so she put her spoon on one and placed the salt and pepper shakers on some others.

"Did you know that this property has a reputation for being haunted?" She was grinning as she spoke.

Everyone looked up from their lunch. Tim gave her the side-eye. "No, I'm afraid I hadn't heard that," he said. "Care to share?"

"Well, over the years there have been various sightings of native Americans appearing and disappearing right around our house."

"Indians?" Tony blurted out with his fork stopped in front of his mouth. "Here?"

"Native Americans, Tony," she replied. "Indians live in Asia. But, yeah. Seems that is the reason this house has had so many owners over the years. People move in, get spooked, then move out. Apparently, that's been the pattern for decades."

"Guess I should have checked this out before I bought it, but how many owners has it had?" Tim asked. He propped his elbows on the table, then thinking better of it, he moved his hands to his lap.

She answered, "This house was built in 1858, which makes it over one hundred and fifty years old. In that time, it's had seventy-five owners and countless other tenants."

"Good grief," Tim said. "I just don't understand that. It's a beautiful old house on a wonderful piece of property." He gazed around at the scenery. The forest surrounded the yard, and rolling hills were visible through a clearing to the west. "I don't understand why anyone would ever want to leave it."

"Unless it's actually haunted," his wife said with a smirk, her dimples appearing.

Tim loved the way the dimples showed up when she smiled. "That would explain it," he said with more than a hint of sarcasm. "No ghost is gonna get me out of here, though. I love this place already." It was true. He loved the forest. He loved the stars he could see without all the lights and noise of the city. There was nothing better than the wildlife that showed up in the early mornings. It just felt good. He felt like he could breathe.

"God is greater than any ghost," Teresa said. "He'll protect us anyway." The rest of the family turned and stared at her like she'd grown a third eye on her forehead. Ignoring their stares, she grabbed her Bible and sprinted off to meet her friend. Over her shoulder she yelled, "The Lord is my shepherd…right? Psalm twenty-three and all." Then she disappeared past the sycamore and around the corner.

Traci peered at Tim. "She's going a little overboard on the Bible stuff, don't you think?"

"She'll be fine," Tim answered. "It's a phase."

Faith and Bible and church had all been a phase for Tim when he was a kid. His parents had dragged him to church every week as a boy until at age thirteen he'd been baptized. He figured he couldn't get around it, so he might as well join the church. Besides, he had friends in the youth group, and they did a lot of fun things. Cincinnati Reds games.

Summer camp. Amusement parks. Things that boys his age loved to do. So, he put on his God clothes and passed through that phase of his life. That is, until he grew up, then reality took the place of spirituality, and God was relegated to whatever time he had left after everything else was done. He couldn't remember the last time he'd picked up the Good Book.

~

Six hours later, the sun was beginning to set in the October sky and the multi-colored leaves were drifting down creating a collage of autumn color that stretched from the still green lawn up through the angled and twisted limbs of the forest. The giant leaves of their home's lone sycamore gathered on the porch and around the rose bushes that formed a prickly barrier between the house and the outside world.

Inside the house, Tim was reading a history book. Teresa was reading her Bible. Tony was driving his Tonka dump truck around the oak floorboards, pulling through tunnels formed by table legs and down highways created by carpet runners. Traci was cooking dinner and gazing out at the beauty of the changing forest before her.

Inspired by the great tree outside the kitchen window, Traci said, "Tim, how tall will the sycamore grow?"

"If I cut it down, you'll never know," he replied with a snicker.

"No way," Teresa exclaimed. "You can't. I love that tree."

Tim ignored her. Tony was oblivious. Only

Traci noticed Teresa's pained expression.

"It's okay, Teresa. He was only joking with me. It's a line from the movie, *Pocahontas*, remember?" Relief swept across her daughter's eyes. Traci turned her attention back to the fading panorama of her new yard and the neighboring forest. Mesmerized by the drifting yellow and orange leaves, her mind floated back to times past when things were simpler for her, times when all she had to do was run and play in the leaves. Running. Laughing. Jumping into raked-up piles. A smile crept across her face as she whipped the milk and butter into the mashed potatoes. For the first time in years, she felt a measure of contentment.

Memories stampeded her mind. Her story. She'd married Tim right after high school and dropped out of college when she became pregnant with Teresa. From then on, it was life on a shoestring, with the constant pressure to maintain the household. The truth was she sometimes doubted her love for her husband. Had she jumped in too young? What might her life have been if she'd waited? In a sense, she envied her daughter, the faith building in her, and Traci yearned for the youthful innocence she once had. Now that they were living in Cutters Notch, away from the need to keep up appearances in Indianapolis, Traci was starting to feel like she could regain a sense of balance in her life. *Maybe*. Looking out the window at the beauty of the falling leaves, she thought, *just maybe*.

That was went she saw it. Just a flash of movement. It darted from behind a bushy, wild honeysuckle and then ducked in behind a large old oak. It was a mere form, a shadow really. But it looked like a man. A man in odd, sort of primitive clothing.

Suddenly, the forest no longer looked beautiful. The sun had drifted lower, and now the shadows were overtaking the fluttering leaves. Darkness was encroaching from every angle, and she remembered the file of old "ghost" stories she'd been reading earlier. She glanced at the file sitting on the counter, one clipping protruding from the side.

Traci shook her head. It was just her unconscious mind playing tricks with her. Her overactive imagination was at work again. It had plagued her at night since she was a small girl, and this was no different. She was a creative at heart, and creatives were blessed with intense imaginations. But she'd learned to use her rational mind to overcome the irrational fears of her creative side.

Then, she saw it again.

This time the figure darted from behind the oak toward the great old sycamore near the house. Long, dark hair flowed out in the wind. She dropped the pan of potatoes and the whipping spoon. They clanged into the sink.

"Tim!" she nearly screamed. "There's an Indian in the yard."

"What?" Tim looked up from his book.

"You mean 'Native American', Mom," Tony said.

Ignoring the boy, she said, "Tim, there a man in the yard. I've seen him twice. He looks like an India…I mean Native American. He's sneaking around and just came up by the house."

"You're just messin' with me," Tim said.

"Trying to get me riled up over those stories you told me. You can stop 'cause it ain't gonna work."

"No," she said. "I mean it. I saw him." She came out from behind the kitchen counter, her eyes darting from window to window.

~

Tim looked at his wife. Genuine fear filled her eyes. As he stood, a thump sounded close, perhaps on the wooden planks that formed the floor of his porch. Now, the situation had everyone's attention.

Two more thumps.

Tim strode directly to the door, threw it open, and stepped out onto the cedar decking. He gasped and stared up at one of the largest men he had ever seen. Standing just to the right of the doorway and silhouetted by the great old tree was an oddly dressed man with long feather-tipped hair, draped in fur and carrying a large spear. His bright blue eyes pierced through Tim with an icy stare that could turn even the hottest oceans of courage into ice.

Tim froze and took a step back. Recovering quickly, he gathered his wits, tried to stand more upright, and confronted the man. "Hey! What do you want?" he demanded. "Why are you sneaking around my property?"

The man stood there quietly. He seemed to be evaluating Tim. His right hand held the spear, but his left hand rested on the hilt of a very large knife. His massive chest rose and fell as he slowly breathed in the evening air.

His hands shaking, Tim pressed on. "Speak, man. What do you want? Why are you here? Do I need to call the sheriff?"

After a few more moments of silence, the huge figure finally spoke, "My name is Tomo. I am the guardian of the stone." He gestured with his spear toward the slab of limestone in the yard. The man's stare didn't weaken, and his hand didn't move away from the knife.

Nevertheless, Tim was determined to show that he was man enough to deal with this apparent threat. Neither man seemed ready to back down. "Okay, Tomo. My name is Tim and I own this place. I'd like you to get off my porch and leave. You've scared my family, and I don't appreciate that."

"You must not move the sacred stone," the man said with a deep monotone voice that seemed to boom from his throat with little effort. "Do not move the stone." As he spoke, he again lifted his right hand and pointed the spear toward the large limestone slab. "My people have guarded that stone for season upon season. It must not be moved."

"Well, Tomo, apparently your job is done. I own that stone now, and it sits where my pool needs to go. I'll be moving it tomorrow."

For the first time, the man's eyes shifted. Interpreting it as hesitation, Tim pressed on. "Now, if you aren't off my property in about thirty seconds, I'm going to do two things. I'm going to call 911, and I am going to get my shotgun. Maybe not in that order."

The focus of the ancient figure's eyes reset upon Tim, and he stepped forward into that uncomfortable space directly in front of the smaller man. Since Tomo was several inches taller, he stared down upon Tim's face. The spear again rested on the surface of the porch, but the tip was above Tim's head. "I warn you. You must not move the sacred stone. It restrains a great evil that must not be released. Long seasons ago, it claimed many of my people, but the Great Spirit has banished it to the depths of Abandon for as long as the stone remains unmoved."

"Traci, call the sheriff," Tim yelled to his wife who was watching the whole thing from the kitchen window. "Look, Tomo, if that is really your name, get off my porch and get off my property. I'm going to get my shotgun, and if you aren't gone when I get back, you'll be picking buckshot outta your butt."

As Tim moved back toward his door, Tomo stepped off the porch decking. "I warn you, you small rooster of a man. Destruction will come to many if you do not heed my words. You must not move the stone." As he said those words, he strode to the far side of the sycamore.

Tim watched him go, and when Tomo didn't emerge past the tree, he raced after him to ensure he kept going. But, when Tim reached the sycamore, the unusual man was nowhere to be seen. Peering around the tree and past the side of the house, Tim couldn't find him. It was almost as if he'd simply stepped off into nowhere.

Sheriff J.B. Dunlap came and went, chuckling at another Indian sighting at the old house. "Probably some local teens playing a practical joke," he suggested, obviously not taking the confrontation seriously. Eventually, the family settled down. It was a restless night, but they tried to sleep. Both Tony and Teresa slept on air mattresses on their parents' bedroom floor. Tim had the shotgun loaded and leaning in a nearby corner. The whole family was on edge.

Sunday morning finally dawned bright and chilly. The family rose to start the day with Traci heading to the kitchen to pull together a breakfast, Teresa snagged the bathroom to perform her beauty rituals, and Tim and Tony slipped outside to answer the call of nature. After all, pressure was pressure, and as nice as the place was, it still had only one bathroom.

As they stepped out the backdoor, the guys were confronted with an astonishing sight. The large stone was encased in hundreds of small stones ranging from three inches to six inches in diameter. Around the stone works, twelve large spears were driven into the ground. Each had feathers and strips of cloth fluttering from the shafts at various heights. Outside the ring of spears was another ring of twelve larger stones, large enough to sit on. On top of the limestone was a small fire, or more accurately, the remnants of a small fire. A stream of smoke still rose from the center.

"Traci, come see this," he called out.

"Whaaa…?" Her question drifted off as her mouth fell open.

"Some prank, huh?" Tim asked with a sarcastic tone. "It's gonna take Tony and me all morning to clear that away."

"What about church?" Teresa asked. She'd slipped out behind her mother. "We've gotta go to church."

"You and your momma can go. Me and Tony will clean this up. We've got to get it done 'cause

Jim's coming over after lunch with the tractor."

"Tim, maybe we should just leave it alone," Traci said. She wrapped her arms around herself in the cold morning air. "I'm kind of freaked out by all this. Maybe it really is a sacred site for Native Americans. Maybe we should let it be."

"Oh, come on, Traci. If it were a sacred site, we'd have been officially notified. It would have been in the purchase paperwork. There wouldn't be a strange guy on our porch or spears in the yard. I'm not sure what the deal really is, but I'm not letting some crackpots keep us from building our pool on our own property."

An hour later, breakfast finished, the girls headed off to church and the guys started carting stones off to the woods. It was almost noon when the last rock was removed. Tim was using a scoop shovel to lift the charred wood off the top when he noticed some shallow markings on the surface. They were so faint that he couldn't easily make out the images, but they seemed very old and weathered. He poured some water over the surface to clean the stone, hoping the pictures would pop out. A large image in the center had eight jagged legs extending around an oval figure. Dozens of smaller figures were scattered around the larger one, some with spears in hand, while others were reclining—or maybe dead.

Showing the figures to his son, he said, "Maybe we do have an old Indian relic here."

"Are we not gonna move it then?" asked the boy. "It would be cool to have something like this in our yard."

"Oh, yeah. We're moving it," he replied. "But

we'll keep it safe in another spot so we can show someone who can make sense of it."

Shortly after noon, Traci and Teresa returned home from church to find Tim sipping lemonade while Tony was trying to throw a spear at the sycamore tree. He was failing miserably to the great benefit of the tree because each spear was almost twice his height.

"Your daughter has a guy interested in her," Traci announced. "You should have seen them sitting together. It was so fun to watch."

"Aw, Mom," Teresa whined and ran inside.

"Great," Tim answered. "Just what we need."

"Yeah, and he's a real cutie too," she snickered.

"Stop it, Mom," Teresa yelled from inside.

"Mom." Tony emerged from his immersion in the art of spear-throwing to see that she had come home. "Dad says we really do have an Indian relic."

"Oh, yeah?" Traci's eyes widened. "Is that right, Tim?"

"Seems so. It's covered with markings that look extremely old. Looks like a drawing of a battle with a giant creature of some sort. Don't know what kind…just has a lot of legs. Have a look."

They walked over together, kicking leaves along the way. More leaves were drifting down, tossed to and fro on the wind. Tim pointed out the ancient designs, tracing the lines with his finger.

"Are you going to leave it alone then?" she asked. "I mean, maybe we should respect Tomo's request, after all."

"First, Tomo didn't make a request. Tomo made a demand. I don't like strange men, dressed in dead animals, showing up on my porch in the dark and making demands. Second, yes, I am still moving it. Jim will be here any minute."

"But—"

"No buts. If we wait until some historian gets wind of this, we'll never be able to move it. I'm gonna move it, but I'm also going to be careful and keep it safe and out of the way. Okay?"

"Well…"

"Look. I promise we won't even scratch it." Tim put his arm around his bride's shoulders. "Seriously. I promise to take good care of it. Besides, it might be worth a bunch of money." A sneaky smile crossed his lips.

"Oh, okay," Traci said. "Just remember your promise."

About that time, Jim Abbott from a couple of miles further south on Robbins Creek Road rumbled into the driveway on his huge green John Deere tractor. He was about as big as a small elephant, but the tractor made him look tiny in comparison. It was convenient to be able to hire out the tractor on occasion, but Tim didn't relish the idea too much because Jim was an unpleasant sort of man. He swore with every breath, smoked huge cigars, and leered at his wife and daughter whenever they were around. He wore bib overalls, a long-sleeved red, flannel shirt, and a camouflage cap with the rebel battle flag emblazoned on the front.

Tim directed him around the house to the stone. When he maneuvered the Deere into position, he shut it down and without a word—at least not a word fit for young ears—he lumbered over to the woods and relieved himself in the brush. He must have been holding a gallon of water because it took him about five minutes to finish the job.

By the time he returned, Tim had secured a chain around the stone and fastened it to the tractor. Mindful of his promise to Traci, he placed a burlap cloth between the chain and the stone to protect it from damage. "Drag it over there by the woods," Tim said. "Take it easy, now, Jim. I don't want the chain to slip. It has some markings on the top I want to protect."

"Got it, Chief," Jim replied. "I'll ease it over like I'm sneakin' past my old lady on a Friday night." As he spoke, he removed his cap and rubbed his forehead with a dirty red bandana that he then re-stuffed into one of his overall pockets.

As the mammoth of a man jumped back up on the mighty machine, the words of Tomo returned to Tim's mind: *I warn you. You must not move the sacred stone. It restrains a great evil that must not be released. Long seasons ago, it claimed many of my people, but the Great Spirit has banished it to the depths of Abandon for as long as the stone remains unmoved.* Along with the words, a hint of doubt arose in the man's mind. *A 'great evil.' What did that mean?*

"Are you ready for me to do this or not?" the coarse neighbor in the rebellious hat demanded. "I got other stuff to do, ya know."

Tim motioned for him to proceed, and then watched with some trepidation as the great stone moved aside. First, the chain grew taunt, and Tim thought maybe it would snap under the weight of the relic, but then the slab began to move. A scraping noise jarred Tim's ears as it shifted.

Soon, it was on its way to its new resting place, and Tim ambled over to look at the spot where it had been stationed for God knows how many hundreds of years. Reaching the place, he stopped short and gasped. "What in the world?" he remarked. "What do we have here?"

Tony had been watching from the porch, his feet dangling off the steps, but now he ran down to join his dad.

"What is it?" he asked as he trotted up beside him. "What's there?"

Tim didn't respond. Rather, he stood there looking at what seemed to be a manhole cover in the earth. It was about three feet in diameter, made of stone, and was covered with hundreds of strange curved markings. They were not the same as the rough drawings on the stone. Rather, the characters wound around the outer rim in a circle. More characters formed rings within the larger ones like age rings in a tree. In the very center was an oval with a circle in the center that gave the impression of an eye.

The circular stone was set in a depression that was only slightly larger in diameter. It was perfectly centered, leaving only about an eighth of an inch of clearance. The base that contained the stone seemed to be formed from marble, while the stone itself had the appearance of granite.

"What the blazes is that, city slicker?" asked Jim, ambling over for a looksee. "Got yerself a well or somethin'?"

"No idea. I think it's too old to be that. Plus, who puts a granite plate over a well? Look at those weird marks."

Tim scratched his chin. Jim scratched his privates. Both men just stared at the strange relic from under the moved slab.

"Tony, go to the barn and get me that old pry bar," Tim instructed.

A couple of minutes later, Tony returned with the tool. Tim took it and then circled the stone, examining it from various angles. Should he lift it or not? He could be unearthing an ancient grave. If that were the case, he'd be in for a world of hurt because he'd have to report it, and that would lead to officials, archeologists, and reporters crawling around. There would definitely not be a swimming pool. The site would require special care, and his property would likely fall into the hands of the government. Still, he was curious—very curious.

Tim was still thinking it over when a whistle interrupted his thoughts, the kind of whistle some men make as an attractive woman walks by—a rude, obnoxious catcall. Teresa, Bible in hand, had stepped out on the porch and Jim was ogling her. He whistled again, his eyes checking her out from head to toe. "Boy, that girl's a hot one," he said with a lustful tone.

"Are you kidding me?" Tim spat out. "Are you going to say that kind of crap right in front of me? I'm her dad, you know. That's my little girl you're talking about."

"Well, I'm not her dad," the supersized man said with a chuckle. "She ain't my little girl. Woo hoo."

"Abbott, I cannot believe you would say something like that. I'm done with you." Tim's face reddened, and he could feel the veins in his neck bulging. It was all he could do not to knock the man upside his oversized head. "You've pushed my last button. I'll pay you, but then get off my property. Got it?"

"Sure enough. Game's on TV anyway. That'll be fifty bucks." He was still casting glances at Teresa on the porch.

"Tony, run in and get this jerk his money from your mom. Tell her fifty dollars."

When the boy had retreated to the house, Tim forced his anger aside and returned his attention to the round stone tablet set in the earth. He made his decision and slipped the pry bar into the slight gap and lifted it. Working carefully, he was able to maneuver the bar further under the lip and slide it over. Once propped on the edge, he set the bar aside and used his hands to push it further off the opening, revealing a dark, deep hole. His eyes couldn't penetrate the darkness to see more than a couple of feet down the sides.

"Tony," he called. "Bring the flashlight from the kitchen drawer when you come back out."

"I got a Maglite here on my belt," the disgusting local tractor driver said, and he handed it over to Tim. "What's down there?"

"I dunno." Tim clicked on the beam, so consumed with the possibilities of the hole that he forgot how disgusted he was with the flashlight owner. "I can't really see anything. It looks incredibly deep."

Tim shone the light into the hole, examining the edges, and running the beam down the cylindrical sides. The appearance of marble along the rim extended into the hole as far as he could see. Perfectly smooth on the sides, the appearance was almost crystalline. Tony returned with the man's money and the other light. He handed the cash to Abbott and then lined up next to his dad. They flashed both beams into the hole and still couldn't see the bottom.

"What do you think's down there, Dad?"

"Shh." Tim dropped a large stone into the abyss. They listened for several seconds but didn't hear it hit the bottom. It was obviously crazy deep.

"What have you done?" boomed a deep voice from behind them. "You have brought disaster upon yourselves and many others as well."

The two men and the boy spun around to see Tomo standing beside the great, old sycamore. He seemed even larger in the daylight, and a look of sheer terror blanketed his face. His left hand trembled as he held onto the ancient tree.

"Quickly, return the cover," he shouted as he ran up to join the trio. "You must replace the lid before he awakens. Perhaps it is not too late. Be quick."

A great and horrible screech erupted from the darkness at their feet. It pierced the tranquility of the autumn afternoon, rattling the windows and causing hundreds of birds to leap into the air from the forest. The screech ended as quickly as it began, but a cacophony of clicking sounds followed, like thousands of fingers tapping a tabletop at once.

Click,   *click,*   *click, clickclickclickclickclickclickclickclick.*

It grew louder, and louder. *Clickclickclickclickclickclickclick.*

"Doom! We are all doomed," Tomo shouted over the noise emitting from the hole. "It is too late to stop him from returning. Run. Run for your lives."

Whipping around, Tim and Tony raced toward the house. Tim glanced back. Jim, slow to move at any time, had not yet comprehended the situation and remained where he was. Tomo joined them and headed toward the old house.

Before they made it more than ten feet, a thick, fibrous fog burst forth from the darkness. Spurting well above the treetops, it spread out into a great dome that enveloped the entire open yard and house. Walls formed on every side that prevented a view beyond that gray membrane in any direction. The previously bright October afternoon was now subdued into what felt like a gloomy overcast winter evening with most of the sun being filtered out.

"Get into your house," Tomo shouted. "Barricade the doors and windows."

Now, even the rude redneck was beginning to move. It was like he was having difficulty overcoming the inertia. His big feet moved like giant pistons trying to trudge through gummy oil.

The fog ceased to flow from the hole, but the clicking sound became even more intense. Louder and louder still. *Clickclickclickclickclickclickclickclickclickclickclick.*

As the two men and the boy reached the back porch, they turned to urge Jim to keep moving. He had only gone a few feet before the clicking reached the surface, and a sea of puppy-sized black creatures swelled over the lip of the hole and scattered in every direction as they poured out. With bulbous abdomens of about a foot in diameter and multi-jointed legs that jutted in every angle, they were a surging storm of huge spiders.

"Inside," Tim ordered his children. He shoved them through the door, immediately followed by the Native American guardian. They turned in anticipation that Jim would be on their heels. Instead, they witnessed two things. First, Jim tripped over the pry bar. Second, the spider horde descended upon him, biting him, and then spinning him into a silk-like cocoon, hanging him from the gray domed walls. His entire body was encompassed except for his face. His mouth was covered, but his nose and eyes were free, his eyeballs bulging in fear.

Tim slammed the door and then ran to close the open kitchen window. He barely slammed it down before black legs scrambled over the glass.

"Quick, make sure all of the other windows are closed," he ordered.

With haste, all the windows and doors were successfully secured, then everyone gathered in the family room. Traci was holding Teresa. Both were shaking. Tony was holding on to his mother's right leg. Everyone was staring at Tomo with a mixture of fear and hopefulness, afraid of what was emerging from the hole and of Tomo's reaction at Tim's disregard of his warnings. At the same time, they all were hoping against hope that the Native American would have some answer to how they might escape with their lives. That hope was quickly dispelled.

"We are doomed," he simply announced. "You have killed us all with what you have done. Us, and perhaps many, many more." He lowered his head and sat on their sofa as if accepting their inevitable fate.

Tim stared out the window. Between the flittering legs, he saw his yard being transformed into a horrific globe of intertwining spider silk which created the largest web that he'd ever seen. As he looked, he saw leering, insulting Jim Abbott suspended in the air. He was hanging from a line that stretched to the domed ceiling, dangling like a deer carcass after the hunt.

The clicking now sounded all around them, echoing from every corner of the house as it was quickly being encased in its own web cocoon.

Clickclickclickclickclickclickclickclickclickclick click.

Tomo began a depressing description of how their lives would end. "Then when he is done toying with us, he will drain our bodies and move on to find other prey," he said as he finished.

Tim twisted away from the window and advanced on him. "Shut up! Just shut up, will you? How was I supposed to know this would happen? Why would I have believed your story? It was crazy."

Stunned, the stone sentry fell silent for a moment. Then, he said, "And yet, you see that I spoke the truth."

"There must be a way out of this," Traci suggested. "How did your people survive?" She knelt down before him, placing her right hand on his large shoulder.

"Most did not," began Tomo. "He claimed nearly our entire clan, and this after he had wiped other clans from the earth throughout our trading area."

"You keep saying 'he'. All I see are huge spiders," Tim said. "What are we missing?" He joined his wife in front of Tomo but declined to take a knee.

"The spiders you see are only his servants," Tomo explained. "He has not yet arisen. He will soon follow. And when he does, we will perish." He lowered his head to his hands. "My people will perish after all." His shoulders shook as he began to cry.

Teresa began weeping, too. She was now sitting on the couch beside Tomo, rocking back and forth, and mumbling a prayer between sobs. Tony had fallen silent and was sitting on the floor with his back to the sofa, leaning to one side against his sister's legs. She wrapped one arm around his neck.

"But Tomo, you obviously defeated him before," Traci pointed out. "There must be a way to live through this. How did your people do it? How did they lock him in and survive?"

He explained, "The Great Evil was once a man, a shaman to a clan that lived nearer where the sun rises. He became obsessed with dark magic, with the ability to manipulate his form and change his body into that of various creatures. One night, he shifted into the form of a small, black spider. While in that form, the wiles of a she-spider seduced him, and as with all female spiders, she meant to have him as a meal in the end."

"Apparently, she wasn't successful," Traci said.

"Before she could finish him, he cast a hasty spell of self-preservation and attempted to revert to human form. It was an imperfect spell that left him trapped between forms, condemned to spend his future as part man and part spider. The result was a raging insanity, and he began to wipe his own people from the earth as he feasted upon the flesh of his family and his clan. Once he had eaten all his own people, he sought out other clans, and soon most of our peaceful people were gone.

"Those of my ancestors who were left gathered here in this place to call upon the Great Spirit to take vengeance upon the Great Evil. They danced and they prayed. They called out in their great fear and desperation. In His great mercy, the Great Spirit heard their pleas. When the shaman found them, the Great Spirit drove him into the depths below this place and held him there while the people fashioned the stones of containment. There he has been kept until your foolishness today. Now, he is free, and we will die."

Tim grabbed his shotgun from the corner, inserted several shells, and pumped a round into the chamber. Pulling aside the curtains, he glanced outside to assess the situation. The web work appeared to be completed, and now a thousand spider eyes were calmly positioned between the house and the hole, staring eagerly at him and his trapped family as if knowing it was only a matter of time.

For the first time, he noticed that a blue luminescence was being emitted from the dark abyss. It was fluctuating light to dark and back again. "The hole is glowing," he announced.

"He is coming now," Tomo replied. "The walls of this wooden and brick abode will not resist him for long," he added as he looked around the room.

Traci was near panic. "Call out to your Great Spirit again. Ask him to spare us. We won't be so stupid again. Please. Ask him to rescue us."

"It is not possible," he answered with a somber glance in her direction. "We have not made the preparations. We do not have the herbs and the fire. We do not have the dancers and the wise men. And above all, I do not know all the words to speak."

The house began to rumble, pictures fell from the walls, lamps rattled on tables, and a crack split a windowpane over the kitchen sink. The blue glow now lit up the entire web dome and leaked into the room, giving everyone an eerie appearance. From outside, there arose a chorus of high-pitched squeals as the minions greeted their master. Inside the home, curiosity drove five sets of human eyes to cluster near the two rear windows to see the sight. Terror consumed any hint of hope.

Standing in the middle of the yard between the house and where the old stone had once been stationed with hundreds, perhaps thousands of squirming spiders swarming around his eight multi-jointed legs was a massive creature with the abdomen of a spider and the torso of a man. The creature's abdomen pulsated with a blue glow. His face, flanked by long, dark hair, was shaped like a human, but he had large, bulbous eyes, and pincers extended from each side of his jaw. He studied the house and the human eyes at the windows, the pincers moving in and out. They turned to point downward, and a smile formed on his lips.

Then, he turned his attention to the large morsel in the cocoon. Jim's head was all that was not fully encased. His camo hat still rested on his fat scalp; its bill extended out of the webbing. Moving so quickly that it was a blur, the monster came up beside the immobilized man. Bringing his huge eyes up evenly with Abbott's terrified pupils, he seemed to savor the moment, and then the pincers sunk deeply into the man's throat. The man-spider then began to drain him. The juices of life visibly flowed through man-spider's transparent pincers until the big man was nothing more than a gunny sack of dry human bones.

"Ahhhhhhh, tasty. It has been so long," the creature's words resounded above the cacophony of minion squeals. "Ah ha ha ha!" He raised his forelegs over his head in joy.

As if the large man were only an appetizer, the insane arachnid turned his attention back to the house. Moving up to the porch, he used his front feet to delicately examine the wood frame, the support posts, and the gutters along the porch roof. "Come out. Come out. Let us discuss your fates." His voice was like the screech of a squeaky hinge. "Come out now and perhaps I may spare some of you. Perhaps, I will be merciful."

"He lies," Tomo said. "He will spare none."

"I am not going to sit here and wait for him to come get us," Tim exclaimed. "I'll see how he likes the taste of buckshot." He lifted the shotgun and reached for the doorknob.

"No!" Teresa screamed. "Don't go out there,

Dad. Don't do it."

Tony latched onto Tim's arm and pulled. Traci tried to block his path to the door. Tim shook them all off.

"Look," he said. "We have two choices. We can sit in here and wait for that thing to tear the walls down and find us. Or, we can take the fight to him. I'm not going to cower in here like a beaten dog. He may kill us, but he'll have to do it the hard way."

"Come out," the man-spider shouted. "Perhaps I will be quick, and you will feel no pain. If you make me work, I will be slow, and you will feel your life slowly drain from your feeble bodies."

Tim looked each member of his family in the eyes and apologized. "I am so sorry," he said. "I love you all so, so much." After a moment of quiet closeness, he glanced at Tomo and opened the door. They nodded at one another.

Stepping outside, he leveled the shotgun at the giant being. Evil intent oozed from the creature, and dread settled in Tim's soul. The air was stale and warm. The only movement was the constant chatter of the spider legs.

"Taste this," he shouted. Then he fired the shotgun into the torso of the shaman. He slid another round into place and fired into the bulbous abdomen. Neither shot had any effect. The pellets made contact but were simply absorbed like rocks into a muddy bog.

"Ah ha ha ha." The man-spider laughed. "Do you think your silly weapon is any match for my magic? You are weak and stupid. Ah ha ha ha. But maybe you are tasty."

From the point at the end of the thing's abdomen, a huge stream of silk burst forth and enveloped Tim. The shotgun flew from his hands and he was pulled from the porch. In seconds, he was strung up next to the remains of the tractor driver. A strand of web gagged his mouth.

Tomo followed Tim through the door, and he began to chant and call on the Great Spirit. He moved rhythmically from side to side.

"Ah ha ha ha," squealed the creature. "You are of my race. How refreshing. I see that you still rely on the words, but you know not the meaning. It is only a ritual to you, and your words are lost on the wind." Another stream of silk grabbed up the guardian and soon he hung next to Tim.

~

From inside, the evil presence could hear Traci trying to pray. She was trying to call up a faith that she hadn't cultivated. She was appealing to the Great Spirit to whom Tomo's people had called upon hundreds of years before.

With a sweep of one massive forefoot, the giant spider swept away a rear wall. Debris flew out and was caught up in the webbing all around. Spotting the praying mother inside, he chuckled. "Your words are also lost on the wind." Then, it snagged her with more silk and strung her up, leaving only Teresa and Tony to face it.

~

The two children huddled in a corner with Teresa shielding her younger brother. She was clutching her Bible to her chest, and with her eyes closed she prayed with all her heart, calling upon her youthful faith.

"Ah. One of innocent faith," the evil one said. "But will that faith save you? We will see." It paused and studied the young girl's words. "But first I think I will test you. I will take your brother before you and drain him while you pray."

"No," the girl shouted. "Leave him alone." She shoved Tony behind her.

"I will take him, and I will eat him first. Sometimes the youngest ones are the sweetest."

"Oh, God. Oh, Lord. Please rescue us," Teresa wailed.

"I will take him slowly. I will sip him like a drink of cool water." He paused again, staring at her. "Unless… Oh, here is an idea. Unless you renounce your faith. If you will admit that your faith is worthless, I will only eat you and spare your brother. Yes, I will do that for you."

"Never," she shouted at the abomination before her. "I will never turn from my God. I love Him completely and I trust in His power." Teresa glared at him, righteous determination making her shiver. "Even if you eat us, the Lord will bring us close to Himself, and you will still be alone in your pain."

The blue light in the man-spider's abdomen turned red, and his eyes focused on her until the hatred was palpable. With no further words, two streams of silk erupted, encasing both Teresa and Tony. They were hung beside the others, and the hateful being surveyed his handiwork. Smirking at the girl, he moved in on her brother.

Using its forelegs, it carefully caressed the cocoon around the boy. "Ah, ha ha ha. Now, you will wish you had taken my suggestion. Now, you will see your brother die."

With its eyes still on her, it moved its pincers into place beside the boy's neck. Moving slowly as it promised, it slid them right up against Tony's throat until they were pressing the skin above his carotid arteries. Tony's eyes were desperate, but spider silk covered his mouth so that he couldn't beg for his own life.

Teresa closed her eyes and prayed one more time. "Please, oh God. Please. You know my heart. You know how much I love you and how much I love my family. Please save us. Please rescue us just like you rescued the Israelites on the shores of the Red Sea, or like you rescued those men in the fiery furnace."

"Your faith is truly a pure and rare thing, but you do not know the right words," said the ancient shaman. "You do not know the songs and the chants that my own people used so long ago. Let us end this. We will end this now." The pincers punctured the boy's neck, but before the creature could take even a tiny taste, another sound rose above the sound of his squirming horde.

A trumpet.

The gloomy web-structured fog split from east to west and was torn aside like a page in a book. In a flash, another being descended, a being dressed all in white. He had wings that extended high above his head, and he carried a sword that gleamed with a brightness that exceeded the light of the sun. Luminescent eyes caught sight of the man-spider, and immediately he struck out with his blade, slicing through the tips of the pincers. He then shoved the creature aside and stood between the thing and the children. The hundreds of smaller spiders fled, spilling into the abyss faster than they had emerged.

"I am a messenger of the Mighty One," declared the rescuer. "The Lord of Hosts has heard the cries of his beloved daughter. The sincerity of her faith and the purity of her love have summoned me here. Now shaman, you will be gone. Go back to the abyss once again. Stay there until that day when you will be called to account. Be gone to the darkness that matches your soul. Be gone now."

With a squeal, the man-spider retreated to the hole, leaving the results of his destruction behind. It slid inside, abdomen first, glaring over the edge of the portal until it fell fully inside.

The angel swept his hand, and the cover plate returned to its spot. He then swept his hand again and the great stone slid across the leaf-covered grass and was repositioned on top. That completed, the angel glided over to Teresa. Staring deeply into her eyes as a refreshing breeze blew through his golden hair, he smiled and the affection he felt for her warmed her heart. "You have done well, young one," he said. "Your love for the Mighty One and your love for your family are evident. You have a bright future because the Lord of Hosts makes all things work out for the benefit of those that love Him. Continue to walk in faith."

His message delivered, he moved to the center of the yard and began to spin. As he spun, a light bloomed from him and the webbing fell free from all the surrounding trees and portions of the home. It was wrapped up into the angel's spin. The fog followed, and an instant later the autumn sunlight returned. All the debris from the destroyed rear of the home reassembled itself. Teresa, Tomo, and the rest of the family fell free from their cocoons. The silken tombs were then swept up into the whirling light. As all returned to normal, the light that was the Mighty One's messenger ascended into the sky until he disappeared from view.

Teresa sat there weeping, holding her brother. Tim, Traci, and Tomo embraced one another above them. Behind them, they heard a rumbling belch. Spinning around, they saw Jim Abbott. The obnoxious neighbor was sitting with his back to the great stone. He was alive and restored.

Obviously dazed, he shook his head and said, "Um, excuse me. I apologize. That was rude." He continued to rattle on a bit. "Um, I'm not sure what just happened, but I'm not feeling real good. I hope you don't mind, but I'm going to get on my tractor and go home." He paused for a moment, then added, "And, I think I'll go to church tonight. Don't know why, but it just seems like a good idea. Maybe I could come back next week and move that rock for you?" he suggested.

"That won't be necessary," Tim replied with a smile. "I've decided not to move it after all." He gazed at each of his family members, and then directly at Tomo. "Instead, I'll make it the centerpiece of a new pavilion. I'll build a roof over it and set it up like a picnic shelter."

Jim struggled to his feet and headed to his tractor, and Tomo approached Tim, Traci, Teresa, and Tony. "Thank you," he said. "I am grateful for your new plan." To Teresa, he said, "I am most grateful for your faith, young one. Your faith has set us free." He lowered his eyes and gave her a respectful bow.

Then turning away, he headed toward that old sycamore tree and said, "I am your friend. And now, you are also guardians of the stone, and I am your guardian as well." Rounding the huge trunk of the great tree, he vanished as if walking through an unseen door.

The family was left sitting together on their lawn, intact despite it all. Fallen leaves blew here and there. The forest swayed in the breeze. The sun formed mottled shadows as it shone down through the crooked branches of the mighty sycamore. And somewhere deep, deep below them, a creature was held captive in the depths of Abandon.

MICHAEL DECAMP

Penny's Pet Peeve

Penny is upset at Donald. In fact, she is completely ticked off at him. It started as a simple pet peeve, like how someone might forget to offer you a drink, or how someone might leave without saying goodbye. Now, however, it has evolved into something much more serious.

Donald has left her all alone again. She hates to be left alone, and jealousy is driving her crazy. He gets to go out every day and see the world in his fancy new car, while she's left to sit at home, staring at the same four walls. Penny's fed up with his lack of concern about what interests her. All he seems to care about is what he wants and what he needs.

At first, it wasn't so bad. Donald would leave for a little while, and she'd miss him, but Penny kind of enjoyed the peace and quiet. Then, she got lonely. The walls seemed to tighten around her. Her imagination contrived all sorts of sounds and shadows that played tricks with her mind. Paranoia grew with each passing day.

When Donald left this morning, he framed Penny's cheeks with his hands and told her he loved her. He said they'd go out for a walk and have a nice talk when he returned home. Talk? Right. As always, he'll do all the talking and she'll do all the listening. It's the same every time. Like an obedient little girl, Penny goes where he wants to go and does what he wants to do.

If he'd ask, she'd tell him she wants to run barefooted through the grass, letting her hair blow in the breeze. New sights and sounds are what she craves. Donald, however, has his own preset course: Up two blocks to the boarded-up school building, across the road, and back past the general store. After skirting the edge of the Cutters Notch park, they're home. He never leaves the sidewalk. The forest surrounds them, but he never considers exploring it. He doesn't even seem to notice the squirrels, the birds, and the wind in the trees.

After squeezing her cheeks and promising the walk, he turned on the TV. "So, you can watch it," he said. That's all she needs, soap operas and lawyer commercials all day long. It seems he feels compelled to control every aspect of her life. Donald tells her what to eat. Donald tells her where to sit. Donald doesn't allow her any visitors.

She's had enough. It's over. Today, she will make it clear that she has feelings and needs and dreams and desires. No more will it be all about Donald. She will take her stand.

It's not like she can't do better. Donald is a simple little man with thinning brown hair and wire-rimmed glasses, and he has put on a few pounds in the time they've been together. She, on the other hand, has been able to maintain her figure despite her living conditions. Her long golden-brown hair still shimmers when sunlight touches it and her legs are toned and strong. She is still young, in shape, and attractive. Without a doubt, she can have any man she wants.

Sure, she's tried to express how she's felt before, but he won't listen. Last week, when he left her alone, she stormed into the bedroom. She threw his clean laundry all over the room, even ripped the bedclothes off the bed thinking that would get his attention off his own little world long enough to realize that she has needs too.

It didn't work. When he came home, he slapped her around until she was a sobbing mess lying in the corner. Penny curled up in a ball and hid her eyes, afraid to look at him. He is so scary when he's mad. Still, it was her fault. She provoked him.

In addition to the beatings and the indifference, Penny is sure he's seeing someone else. She can smell her on his clothes, and she found a long blond hair on his jacket sleeve. Donald claims Penny is his one and only, but the signs are all there. He's probably with her right now, and that's why he's left Penny all alone again. He can play the field, but she's stuck, imprisoned within the same four walls every day.

This time will be different. She's had enough of this purgatory he calls home. She'll make him pay, then leave to make her own life, apart from Donald. So, she waits, watching the door, listening for the sound of his engine and his footsteps on the walk. It will be good; he'll be expecting her to run over and greet him with a kiss like always. He'll want her to shower him with attention, then slink away so he can watch the evening news. Well, not this time. This time she'll surprise him, and everything will change.

Minutes turn into hours, and Penny loses track of time. She's still sitting there watching and waiting when Donald pulls into the driveway late in the afternoon. The evening sun is glaring through the front windows. Penny's pet peeve has turned into anger, then into fury. Her eyes are fiery embers waiting for him to enter.

He shuts off the engine and steps to the walk. The muscles in her neck tense as he approaches the door. She's so ready to show him that living life is important to her, too.

This is her moment. Life will be different from this day forward. No more long days all alone in this hot little house. No more taking orders from this pig of a man who cares so little for her feelings. Her opportunity has arisen, and she's determined to take advantage of it. It's either now or never.

The key turns in the double-sided deadbolt lock, and she prepares herself for action. Every sense is heightened. Every muscle is taut. Every nerve ending is sharpened. The hair stands on the back of her neck. Another second or two and he will pay.

The latch gives and the knob turns. She's crouched, ready behind the wall that separates the entry from the living room. Usually, she greets him at the door. He likes that. Not today.

Donald steps inside, announces his return like a king, and glances around. "Penny, where are you?"

Penny emerges from behind the wall and leaps at him. She catches him off guard, knocks him back through the front door, and he falls to the ground. Standing over him, she bares her teeth and glares into his frightened blue eyes. It's too easy. She could rip the life right out of him.

After a moment, she lowers her snout and simply licks him across the mouth. Then, she bounds across the road, through the park and into the forest.

Penny is finally free, as all dogs should be.

MICHAEL DECAMP

Linda's Window

Bowen County Deputy Calvin Churchill was off duty and mowing his yard in the hot, summer sun when Linda Lawson pulled into the driveway of the house next door. He hadn't seen her in nearly twenty-five years, and even then, it was only in passing. The emotions he felt for her were strongly mixed—still smitten with her, and yet still broken by her. That mixed bag of human internal drama went back further, close to forty-five years. It went back to the time when she wrapped him around her little finger before plunging an icepick into his heart.

Calvin glanced at his ragged cargo shorts and stained t-shirt. A ratty ballcap sat on his head and sweat was soaking his brows. He even had clippings clinging to his arms and legs. As fast as he became self-conscious, he countered the thought with anger for even caring. "Razzlesnatz," he muttered to himself.

Calvin had lived in his little bungalow on Rock Street across from the Cutters Notch Park pretty much all his life. Sure, he'd moved out when he graduated. He'd completed his military service and then had his own place for a few years. But when his parents had grown too old to maintain the house, he moved back and cared for them until their passing, his dad had been gone ten years and his mother five. He'd never married, and he lived in the little house all alone. He still slept in his childhood bedroom.

He figured Linda was here to begin the process of cleaning out her parents' home. The older Lawsons had moved to a senior care facility a couple of weeks back, their place vacant now.

Linda and Calvin, the same age, had been childhood buddies. As little kids, they ran the neighborhood together, but as they grew older, things began to change. Calvin withdrew more into his own head, writing stories in his mind and making up words. Linda, ever the extrovert, became popular which expanded her world. Still, they remained friends—at least until the spring of their senior year in high school.

Calvin had always wanted their relationship to be more, but she intimidated him. He was always afraid she'd reject him. He loved it when she was around. Sometimes, they'd sit together on one or the other's porch late into the evening sipping on a Coke and talking about random stuff. He always wanted to reach over and take her hand, but he just couldn't get up the nerve.

As he remembered those old days, he continued to mow the lawn, even as Linda gathered her things and climbed out of her car. From the corner of his eye, he could see her standing there looking at him. She was probably waiting for him to notice her. Calvin refused to give her what she wanted. Rather, he kept his head down and his eyes focused on the grass.

Even so, he could see from the corner of his eye that she still looked good. Her brown hair was fashionably styled. A touch of makeup brightened her features, but not enough to look gaudy. Plus, she'd kept her figure. Calvin had heard that she'd eventually married, but he was pretty sure the marriage ended a few years back.

Linda stood there and watched him work for several minutes, but when he didn't acknowledge her presence, she turned and went into her parents' house. Only then did Calvin pause and glance over. He regretted that a part of his heart was still attached to that woman.

~

The Cutters Notch Post Office sat on the west end of town. It had been built by the Federal Government in the middle of the 1940s, right after World War II. That was also the last time it had been updated.

It was a small, nondescript, limestone building with a low roof. A wooden ramp, added in the 1990s, led to a small, concrete stoop. The door, centered on the front of the facility, sported a screened, aluminum storm door. The security door hung open on the inside. At the same moment that Linda caused Calvin's internal conflict, voices leaked out the front of the postal facility.

"We're going to move this cabinet into the back room," James Mills, the local postmaster was explaining to his two teenage boys. "We've finally been approved for some new paint in here, and we have to get everything—even this thing—out of the way. This place hasn't been painted since they built it."

The boys had been helping him move furniture and fixtures all morning. He'd point to something and tell them where to put it. They did the heavy lifting, complaining the whole time.

"Is this the last cabinet, Dad?" Jimmy, his oldest boy, asked. "We got stuff to do, too."

His other son was wise enough to keep his mouth shut.

"Just for that, no. I have a whole list of other things for you to do today." James smiled at his son.

"Ugh," the boy groaned. "Okay, I'm sorry."

"Good. Then, let's get this thing moved. Remember to lift with your legs. This is probably the heaviest thing in the building." *I don't think it's been moved since they brought it into the office back in the forties.*

The cabinet itself was solid oak, with drawers in the bottom and dozens of mail slots on the top. The whole thing was built in one massive section. There was no way to disassemble it, so it had to be moved in one piece. James was really curious about what he'd find behind or under it when his boys moved it out of the way.

He watched his offspring position themselves on each end. They bent at the knees and gripped the cabinet, pulling the bottom draws out enough to slip their hands inside. *It's a good thing they're football players and weightlifters or I'd never find anyone to move this thing.* The boys let out a collective grunt as they engaged the weight. To James' amazement, they hoisted it in the air and began to maneuver it into the back room.

After guiding them through the door and pointing out where the cabinet needed to rest, the postmaster returned to examine the paraphernalia that had collected over the decades behind the behemoth piece of oaken office furniture. He scanned the floor at the base of the wall and saw all sorts of papers—circulars and advertisements, some dating back a half century. James was intrigued. He found furniture store ads that announced bedroom suits for fifty dollars. In another ad, he read that you could buy a new Chevy for fourteen hundred dollars. *This is just incredible.*

He was perusing through a grocery store ad from 1965 when he spotted the envelope, a lone piece of personal mail that hid in the errant stash. He picked it up. The envelope was the size of personal stationery. When he turned it over, the postmark read May 1973. It was addressed to Linda Lawson, 1245 Rock Street, Cutters Notch, Indiana. It was from C. Churchill, 1247 Rock Street, Cutters Notch, Indiana.

"C. Churchill," he muttered. "That has to be Calvin." James Mills had been the postmaster for twenty years, so he knew Calvin well. "Linda Lawson? Hmm." He'd known the Lawson couple, but the wife's name wasn't Linda. The husband's name was Frank, and her name was Carol. "I wonder if this is their daughter." He'd been handling their mail for years, and it was a small town. The name "Linda Lawson" did ring a bell, but he'd never met the couple's family. *I wonder why Calvin bothered to mail it to the house next door.*

"Boys," he called out, "Let's go. I have a stop to make on the way home." *It's about time this letter got delivered.*

~

Calvin finished up, put his mower away, and went inside to shower. As he trudged up the back walk, he saw a mail truck parked behind Linda's car. He couldn't get the woman out of his head no matter how hard he tried. Instead, his disobedient brain kept returning to that May in 1973.

They were seniors in high school. Prom was coming up. They were sitting on Linda's porch at eleven o'clock at night. Calvin leaned his back against one of the support posts and was admiring her in the dim light.

She was staring back as she tipped her Coke bottle up for a sip. "Cal," she said with a little smile. "Are you going to the prom?"

"Probably not," he answered. "I don't have a date. How about you?"

"I don't know," she said. "I don't have a date yet, either."

"What about that one boy? What's his name? Bill?"

"Oh, we're done. He's too wild," Linda added. "I like boys who are quiet and thoughtful. Boys who think more than they talk. Kinda like you."

When she spoke those works, a spark broke forth inside Calvin's heart. Suddenly, he allowed feelings that had been suppressed to spring to life. *Is she talking about me? Does she like me for more than just a friend?* He wasn't sure.

"In fact," she continued, "there is one particular

boy that I was sorta hoping would ask me, but he hasn't yet." She kept staring at Calvin, smiling.

Calvin's heart was racing. He wanted to blurt out an invitation to the prom right then and right there, but his insecurities wouldn't let him. He was too doubtful, too unsure. *What if she laughs and says that it was some other boy she had in mind? What if I'm wrong?* He questioned himself right into a frozen state of indecision. That mental logjam remained, and he eventually went home without taking the chance.

Later that night, as he sat at his little desk in front of his bedroom window, he came up with a plan. He could see the light that illuminated Linda's bedroom window across from his own. As kids, they often called out to each other through those windows, sometimes talking into the night before they grew old enough to sit on each other's porches. As he looked at the light from her window, he decided that he needed to push himself. He needed to take a chance. He needed to take his shot. Maybe he couldn't say the words out loud, but he could write them down. He would write her a letter.

For two hours, he poured out his heart. Calvin told her just how he felt about her. How he knew they were best friends, but that he had been in love with her since sixth grade. He told her how he loved her smile and the shape of her nose. How her slender fingers made him want to hold her hand. Everything he'd bottled up, Calvin poured out on the paper on his desk. He was still writing when the light clicked off in her window.

When he finished, Calvin stuffed the letter in a

matching envelope and sealed it up. After addressing it, he placed it on his nightstand. The next morning, he made a beeline to the nearest mailbox and stuffed it inside before he lost his nerve.

Then, he waited for her response. First, he waited with excited expectation for the next day when he knew it would be delivered. Then, he waited an extra day because sometimes things take a little longer than you expect. He saw her sitting out on her porch, but he was too scared to walk over and join her. After a few days, his expectation turned to trepidation, then humiliation as the days began to drift by. She never responded.

The prom passed and she never said a word to him about his letter, no response at all. He was so embarrassed that he could never bring himself to go sit with her again. Instead, he withdrew. Linda called, but he wouldn't come to the phone. She waved, but he acted as if he didn't see her. Eventually, they both graduated. He joined the Air Force and she went off to college.

The decades passed. She married, had a couple of kids, and then her husband cheated so she divorced him. Or, so he'd been told. Calvin spent four years in the military, then moved back home. The dating options were few in Cutters Notch, and he simply never connected with anyone the way he had with Linda. He couldn't get over her. Now, he was close to retirement and all alone.

Calvin showered, shaved, splashed on some cologne out of habit, and slowly dressed. He was still unwillingly thinking about that letter and the way he asked her to respond. He wandered over to his old bedroom window and looked outside.

~

Linda Lawson was sitting at her mother's kitchen table looking through some old pictures when the doorbell rang. She could see Cal pushing the mower back and forth in the neighboring yard. Her heart ached. She just didn't understand what happened between them. She missed him so much; she always had.

Linda could still remember that last time they sat outside together. He leaned back against the post, looking so handsome. Her grin locked in place. It was kind of weird in that she always seemed to smile when he was around, and she couldn't not do it. The way that she saw him had begun to change in the previous months. He'd always been her best friend, but suddenly she found herself attracted to him. Calvin had the qualities she liked. He was good-looking, but he was also kind, thoughtful, and smart. She'd come to realize that he meant more to her than just a friend.

On that night sitting on that porch, while sipping her pop and smiling incessantly, she decided to give him a hint or two. When she saw his reaction, she was sure her hint had gotten through. Still, he didn't say anything. And after that night, he never came out and sat with her again. Instead, he'd grown cold and distant. Instead of lighting the fuse of a beautiful relationship, it seemed that she'd destroyed what they had. It broke her heart.

Ding dong.

Linda opened the front door to a pudgy, middle-aged, balding man standing there in a USPS uniform with a yellowed envelope in his hand.

"Would you happen to be Linda Lawson?" the postal carrier asked. He was wearing a bit of a grin. "Did you live here in 1973?

"Well, yes," she replied. "That is me. How can I help you?"

"Ms. Lawson, we were moving some old furniture around in our post office this morning, and I found this old letter from a long time ago. It's addressed to you, but it was never delivered. It's from May 1973."

Hesitantly, Linda took the envelope from the man's hand, and after thanking him, she returned to the table. Staring at the envelope, she could see it was from Calvin. *From over forty-five years ago?* She squinted at the date. It was around the time when he grew so cold to her. Jumping from the table, she rushed into the kitchen to find something to cut the seal on the letter.

Ten minutes later, as she read the last line, she was sobbing. Tears pooled onto the table below her chin. Her mascara smeared onto her cheeks. It all made sense now. She finally understood. He'd placed all his hopes into the words on those handwritten pages, but the letter never reached her. He thought her answer was no. He'd been heartbroken.

Now, she was heartbroken, too.

She knew what she had to do. Linda jumped to her feet and searched around until she found the supplies she needed. Then, she did it. It was nearly half a century late, but she did it.

~

When Calvin glanced over at the Lawson house, it almost didn't register at first. He did a double-take. What he saw was still there when he looked again. A big white piece of paper hung in Linda's old bedroom window with three giant red letters boldly printed for him to see.

YES!!!

His mouth dropped open. In the letter, his last line was, "If you will go to the prom with me, then put up a sign in your window in red letters." That sign never appeared back in May 1973. It was there now, though. He looked further. There was a sign in every window on that side of the Lawson house. Calvin looked down and Linda was taping one on the side window of her car.

"Raaazzlllesnatz!" he blurted through the massive grin that he felt appear on his face. Then he bolted to the door.

~

Calvin and Linda stared at each other from ten feet apart. He stood barefoot on his freshly cut lawn and Linda stood beside her late model Ford Mustang. It was the first time Calvin had allowed himself to look directly at her in over forty years. He liked what he saw.

Linda was gazing back, the letter in her right hand. Her makeup was smeared, but she was laughing between sobs. "I just received your letter, Cal," she said. "Just now. All these years later. They just delivered it today. I'm so sorry."

"I've really missed you, Linda," he replied. His eyes were moist.

"I've missed you, too, Cal. I really have. So, so

much."

"Did you like the letter?"

She laughed out another sob. "Oh, yes! Very much so. It must have been hard for you to write."

He laughed then. "Uh, yeah. You could say that."

Linda made the first move. She crossed the invisible barrier that divided her parents' driveway from Calvin's yard and took his hand into her own. "Come on," she said. "Let's go over and sit on my porch for a bit. I'll get us a couple of Cokes from the house."

Calvin smiled big. He blushed a little, and the smile wouldn't go away. Inside, his long-broken heart finally mended as her fingers interlaced with his own. "I'd like that," he answered her. "I'd like that a whole lot."

Davy's Gift

December 23

Davy was smart for a seven-year-old. So smart in fact, that he'd advanced way ahead of his first-grade class at the Cutters Notch Elementary school located down the road, just east of town on Highway 257. He could read on a third-grade level already and write nearly as well. Those skills gave him an idea as he lie in his bed, listening to his parents argue downstairs.

The lights were off in his bedroom, all of them except for the closet light. He left it on with the door cracked just to give himself a little bit of light. The wind was blowing outside, and sleet was pelting his second-floor window. The limbs of the huge hickory and elm trees brushed the windows and rain gutters, screeching as they slid one way and then fell back again. The wind pushed against the wooden slat-board siding causing the house to creak and pop, giving it a creepy feeling in the cold night. He could hear every sound the house made, even above his parents' screaming, but he wasn't afraid. Davy was just sad.

He paid attention and had learned details about his new hometown. His house sat on the main street in the town. At one time, the little village of Cutters Notch was a boomtown with funds from the limestone mines filling people's pockets. Now, those days were in the past, the mines were nearly gone, and much of the money had dried up. At night, darkness shrouded the house, aided by the dozens of trees and even more bushes and shrubs. They blocked all the bright lights from the convenience store down on the corner. Only moonlight seeped through his window, and on a sleety night like this, which would soon to be followed by snow, even the moon was kept at bay.

There were similar old houses hidden behind their own trees and shrubs on each side of Davy's house. There weren't any other kids, though. Elderly people occupied the other houses; they probably spent their days tending gardens in the summer. Since it was winter, he imagined them huddled up in front of their TVs. His folks had moved into their rented home about a month earlier, so he hadn't had a chance to meet them yet.

He had no friends nearby. He had no siblings. At night, when his mom and dad fought, Davy was all alone with his thoughts. That was when the sadness crept into his room and cuddled up next to him. Sometimes, he blocked it out by playing imaginary games with his toys. Other times, he just cried.

Davy made a decision, as he lie there listening to the mean words that wafted up the stairs like smoke and seeped in under his bedroom door. He threw back his Batman bedcovers and sat up on the side of his bed. *That's a great idea*, he thought. *I'm gonna do it!*

He found his Spiderman slippers with the help of the wedge of light shooting past his cracked closet door. He put them on and stood. The slippers didn't quite match his Christmas pajamas, but that couldn't be helped; he couldn't expect his mom to give him Christmas PJs and Santa slippers too. With the warm house shoes on his feet, he tiptoed across the hardwood floor, turned on the small lamp on his little desk, and took out a pencil and paper.

He didn't need to worry about getting in trouble for being up late. When his folks argued, they rarely even noticed that he was around. They had their own world. The rest of the universe, him included, disappeared around them. The previous night, when they started up the nightly battle, he'd slipped out on the landing and watched them. They didn't even notice he was there as they hurled their insults and accusations.

They were so angry, their faces turned red and scary. They used words he wasn't allowed to use, and he was sure they fought because of him. He'd seen their happy faces in the pictures on the fireplace mantel, pictures of just the two of them before he'd come along. Davy never personally saw that happiness in their eyes, so he figured he must have caused them to hate each other. It must be his fault. He watched them for a while, listened to their harsh words, and cried because he caused them so much pain. Then he slipped back down the hall.

The previous night, he'd retreated to his secret place. At the back end of the hall, away from the front stairs was a closet. Behind the old coats and extra clothes his mom had stored inside, a small set of steps led up to the attic. Dad was too preoccupied with work to even know about it, and his mom was too creeped out to go up there. So, without his mom even being aware, Davy made the attic his special retreat. His fort. His hideout. It was the one place he could go to escape the battle below, and he sometimes went up there when he couldn't take the pain of it all anymore.

Tonight, though, was different. Tonight, he had an idea, a plan. Perhaps, he could ask for some help. Maybe, in this special season, there was a special person that could make a difference. Possibly, he could help his mom and dad love each other again; maybe he could make his parents love him too. Christmas was just over a day away, and maybe Santa could work some magic.

Sitting down at his desk, Davy called upon everything his teacher had taught him and he wrote the best, most heartfelt plea that his seven-year-old mind could conjure. He started writing it several times but messed up and tore up the pages. It had to be just perfect, so he wadded the papers up and tossed them in the Superman trash can in the corner. After about an hour, with his parents still fussing below him, Davy was satisfied that he got it right and carefully tore out the good page. Folding it in half, he wrote "*Santa*" on the outside and placed it on the corner of his dresser.

Davy glanced up and stared at his own sad reflection in the mirror. The huge piece of reflective glass was mounted on top of the heavy, oak clothing chest on which he had placed the folded letter. *Maybe Santa really can help.* Feeling a little spark of hope, he turned away and went back to bed. Hopeful that he'd struck upon the right idea, he rolled over, curled up in a ball, and put his extra pillow over his head to muffle the noise from below.

Soon, he was asleep. With his back to his dresser, his mind drifted into an anxious dream, where he was running with uncooperative feet from something that he was afraid of but couldn't quite see. During his dream, he didn't notice the odd little hand that emerged from his mirror.

At first, it was just like fingertips poking through plastic wrap, but then an entire hand and arm popped into his room. It came through the glass at the same spot where his face had been reflected just a few minutes earlier. The hand reached in, picked up Davy's letter to Santa, and then slipped back through the surface.

December 24

Hours later, Davy's mother shook him awake, rustled him into the bathroom, and then rushed him through breakfast. He'd barely finished his Captain Crunch, when she hustled him to the car. His dad was already at work, and his mom had plans for them to visit family in Anderson. Davy was so busy with all the driving, eating, presents, and laughter that he forgot all about his special letter. He played with cousins, sat on his grandpa's lap, and ate his grandma's yummy food. It was such a full day that he fell sound asleep on the three-hour drive home.

It was dark outside when he felt the engine shut down. Davy opened his eyes and found himself in his own driveway and saw his dad's Impala through his mom's car window. Snow was starting to fall in huge flakes as they hurried up the sidewalk to the back door. Davy was so full of joy from the great day and excited to see his dad that he ran ahead and banged through the back door. He found his dad sitting at the kitchen table, eating a sandwich and sipping a Coke.

"Dad," he said. "We had the best time. All my cousins were there, and Grandma made a huge dinner. It was so fun."

"Where's your mother?" his dad asked. His voice sounded gruff and he didn't even look up from his sandwich. Davy's smile faltered.

"She's comin'," the boy answered. "Dad, it's almost Christmas and it's snowing too." Davy tried to hang on to the joy that seemed to be slipping away.

Davy's dad ignored his son's excitement and glared over the boy's head at his wife who'd just come through the door.

"I've worked all day while you've been playing, only to come home to a dark house with no dinner," he said with an angry tone. "So, here I am sitting alone, and you've given no thought to me at all. Thanks a lot."

"I just took Davy to my folks' to celebrate Christmas," she replied. "I told you last night we were going. You know my family gets together every year on Christmas Eve."

"And I told you that we couldn't afford the gas."

"That's crap and you know it," she shouted. "Not everything is about you, Brian."

And, they were off to the races with another fight. Soon, they were oblivious to Davy on Christmas Eve as they fussed, fought, argued, and cussed. Hateful, thoughtless words filled the house, echoing off the cavernous walls. Their angry shouts filled every crack and crevice. Davy's excitement over his day with his grandparents, the snow, and Christmas quickly evaporated, replaced by a heaviness, a depression that pulled on his spirit like an anchor tugs on the bow of a ship.

Davy escaped the kitchen, passed through the dining room, and then stopped in the living room in front of the Christmas tree. The tree lights were twinkling off and on against the various shiny bulbs and ornaments, and he thought the tree looked wonderful. Electric candles lined the windows and the fireplace mantle, illuminating the stockings. His mother had even strung electric lights around the window frames and the one mirror that hung on the north wall. The entire room was aglow, creating the impression that the old walls themselves were giving off light. Wires snaked down the walls and wiggled together into a series of extension cords that connected into the three ancient wall sockets scattered at various points above the baseboards. It was his mother's Christmas room. The rest of the house was his father's, but this room belonged to his mom.

"You and the boy go play all day, and I get nothing," his father boomed in the kitchen.

"You call him 'the boy'? Are you crazy?" his mother responded. "He's your son and it's Christmas for God's sake. It's a special time for him."

"Him, him, him! Is it all about him? What about me? Do you save anything for me?"

Davy trudged up the steps toward the second floor, waves of anger passing over his head. The very air in the house felt like it was crowding around him, squeezing him, threatening to drown him. He decided that he couldn't stand to listen to it tonight, so he passed his room and entered the hallway closet. Sliding past the old coats, he could smell his mother's perfume and his father's cologne lingering on the worn fabric. He liked that smell. It smelled like happiness.

Stepping over a couple of cardboard boxes, he mounted the first step. He clicked on the light at the back, revealing the darkly stained, small, steep wooden steps leading toward the ceiling. At the top, he opened the door and entered his sanctuary.

It was a little chilly up in the attic because there weren't any heat ducts providing any furnace air, but he didn't mind if he could escape the noise of hatred below. Between the two doors and the old coats, his secret place was fully insulated from those hurtful words. Scattered around were relics of another age. Boxes of pictures detailing some unknown family's history. Old trunks full of clothes that seemed like the costumes they sometimes used in his school plays. He'd explored it all.

Near the back wall, just to the right of a four-pane window which didn't open, was a large, stand-alone mirror. It was so big that Davy could see his whole body, head to toe. It was nearly as big as their front door. He liked to stand in front of it and make funny faces. Sometimes, he'd put on the old clothes and look at himself, giggling.

In this space, he could pretend. He could imagine that he was someone else, somewhere else. He could be Spiderman slinging webs from rafter to rafter. He could be Superman flexing his muscles of steel. On this night, though, he simply sat down on the floor with his back to the huge mirror and fiddled with some tiny Hot Wheels cars. He'd found them in an old shoebox tucked into a corner. Davy pretended that the lone light strung from the highest point above his head was the sun, and the shadows it cast around him were the forests that surrounded this little town in which he was imprisoned. He pulled out two cars, one for his mom and one for his dad, and began smashing them together, making the sounds of screeching wheels and the booms of crashes.

~

Downstairs, April and Brian carried on in the kitchen. He claimed that she "always" did this or that. She claimed that he "never" did that or this. Was she seeing someone else? Was he married to his job? Accusations disguised as questions flung with animosity and aimed at the heart were fired back and forth. Neither took notice of the time. Neither considered where their boy had gone. They were so consumed with their mutual fits of rage that nothing else in the world penetrated their little vocal boxing ring that doubled as the kitchen.

December 25

They were still so preoccupied with their fussing at midnight that the electrical fire, which erupted from the overloaded circuits in the living room, fully engulfed the front end of the house and crawled up the stairs before they noticed the smoke.

April noticed it first and screamed for Davy. Brian sprinted through the dining room but was blocked by the flames and smoke. He turned and grabbed April who was still screaming for her son.

"DAVY!" she bellowed. "DAVEEEEEY! Oh, God. DAVEEEY!"

Somewhere in the house, a smoke alarm began to screech.

Grabbing his cell phone, Brian dragged April out of the house and called 911. Once outside, he left his distraught wife on the front walk staring at the flames that were blooming in all the front windows, and then ran around to the rear where he stored his extension ladder. Leaning it against the side of the house, Brian scrambled up to Davy's window. In the distance, sirens began to wail. Since it was a small town, fire trucks would be here quickly, at least the guys on duty would. The rest of the volunteers would show up from their various homes as quickly as they could. Brian couldn't wait for them.

When he reached the window, he tried to muscle it up, but it wouldn't budge. Blowing snow assaulted his face and ice numbed his fingers. Using his hands to shield the sides of his face, he peered inside, but couldn't see anything. With no other option, he used his elbow to break the window. Inside, the new source of fresh air caused the fire to leap fully onto the second floor.

The thick, black smoke rushed through Davy's bedroom door and billowed past Brian, making it impossible for him to see anything. Reaching inside the broken window, he unlocked the glassless frame and pushed it up.

"Davy? Davy, can you hear me?" He screamed into the blackness.

No answer.

"Davy? Where are you?" Desperation gripped his heart.

Brian ducked under the acrid smoke and then crawled into his only son's room. Staying low, he crept to the bed. Empty. He checked underneath. No one. He belly-crawled to the closet. Again, empty. By now, he was choking and had to retreat. For the first time, he felt powerless. Where was Davy? Without any clear idea of where else to look, and with poisonous fumes eating at his consciousness, he struggled back through the window and onto the ladder. He slid down the aluminum extension rails and ran back around to April.

She looked at him with hopeful eyes. He looked back with despair. For the first time in months, they embraced one another as firemen raced past them dragging hoses and various other pieces of equipment. Flashing lights bathed them in a pulsating red as they stood there holding one another—helpless.

"My son's in there!" Brian screamed to the passing firemen. "He's somewhere in the house."

~

Davy had fallen asleep on an old quilt in front of the great mirror. He had found the homemade blanket in a box labeled "grandmother," and it made him feel good to pretend that it was from his own grandma, so he made himself a little bed and eventually drifted off.

The fire had been going for quite a while before

the smoke began to penetrate his attic retreat. Eventually, it seeped under the door and up through cracks and crevices that otherwise no one would ever notice. Hugging the floor like a snake looking for a mouse, it drifted back until it found the boy's nose.

Roused by the unpleasant smell, Davy sat up and gasped. He was old enough to remember the stories of house fires on the news, and he'd already been through several fire drills at school. Jumping to his feet, he ran to the door leading through the closet back to the main part of the house, but when he opened it, smoke filled the small area inside. It immediately plumed into the attic, making it hard for him to see and catching in his throat. Scrambling over the boxes and past the coats, he gripped the doorknob to the second floor. It was hot to the touch and burned his hand.

Davy knew he was trapped.

He retreated to the attic. Closing the door, he used some of the old clothes to stuff into the space at the bottom to block out some of the smoke, and then he slowly stepped backward until he felt the smooth glass of the mirror against his butt. There he stood, alone and afraid, watching the smoke slowly fill the room, hoping with all his heart that his mom and dad were safe. He was sure that he would never see them again.

~

Outside, driven together by the terror of potential loss, Brian and April stood holding one another. The veil lifted from their eyes and they recognized one another again. More so, they could see themselves with clarity, a clarity that only guilt could restore.

More equipment arrived every few minutes, and a large tanker truck with shiny chrome panels like large mirrors came to a stop behind them. Large spotlights lit up the whole yard. They watched as men in heavy tarp-like jackets broke their windows and sprayed streams of water inside. Other men kicked open their front door and did the same. The local chief approached and asked if everyone was out.

"Our son is missing," Brian yelled above the noise of the truck's big engine. "We don't know where he is in the house. I put up a ladder and crawled in his room, but I couldn't find him."

"Please save our son!" screamed April. "Please! You've got to find him." She repeated, "Oh, God." And then, she slumped against Brian's chest. He wrapped her in his arms.

Turning away, the fireman lifted his radio and spoke with urgency. Around the house, men moved with what seemed to be more diligence than before, carefully but with measured speed. Two men hurried past them with a large fire ladder. Flames were breaking out of the upstairs windows.

Brian and April, who just a few minutes before were intent on outdoing one another's hurtful words, were now huddled together, each saying a private prayer. Each was promising God that they would change if only he would save their little boy, the little boy that meant the world to them. After all, he was their bright light, their joy amid the chaos of life.

~

In the attic room, Davy was coughing uncontrollably. The light above his head had gone out, and the smoke was so thick he could feel it enveloping him. The only thing he could see was the jumping yellow of the flames as they worked their way through the cracks around the door. The fire was slipping around the top molding of the doorframe and had begun to work its way to the ceiling.

Davy sat on the quilt, the one he imagined to be

his own grandmother's, trying to get low enough so he could still breathe. He pulled a corner of the blanket across his face. The end was near for him, he knew, so he asked God to do what Santa didn't get to do. He asked God to find a way to make his parents happy again.

That prayer made him feel safe despite the smoke and the flames. His mind was growing fuzzy, but it almost seemed to him that God was giving him a hug, and that he was drifting away. He was safe and floating off in someone's strong arms, away from the smoke and through a tunnel to a nice place. There was a face there. A nice face, warm and soft. Friendly eyes.

Then, all was dark.

~

Standing in front of the tanker, Brian and April watched as the firemen seemed to fight a losing battle with their house. The fire was shooting through all of the second-floor windows and was curling up over the roof line. The flames illuminated the surrounding trees causing shadows to dance in the underbrush. Flashing lights, alternating red and white, added to the spectacle, and sirens sounded as other fire departments sent crews to assist.

With each passing moment, their hopes sank deeper and deeper. They watched the men moving into and out of the house, wishing Davy into each man's arms to no avail. The grim look on the firefighters' faces spoke volumes, and they felt the loss of their son with each passing moment—the loss and the guilt of knowing it was their own fault.

"What have we done, Brian?" April choked out as she sobbed into his chest. His own face was streaked with tears. He had no words. For the first time in a long time, he saw himself for what he was—a self-absorbed, insecure, angry man. He had done this. It was truly his fault.

From behind them, near the mirror-like chrome panels of the fire department's red tanker, a booming voice called out, "Here is your son."

Brian and April spun around to see a small, older man with bright, friendly eyes and a short white beard. He was a little odd-looking, and both of his ears seemed to be slightly pointed on the top. All that mattered, though, was that he was holding their son in his arms. Without hesitation, they took Davy from the man and rushed him to the paramedics. There a man put an oxygen mask on Davy's face and hustled him off to their truck.

Assuming the old man to be a neighbor who had come to their boy's rescue, they thanked him profusely. Then, they turned together to follow the medics.

"I suppose your presents have all been lost in the fire," the old man said from behind them.

"Yeah, yeah," answered April, "but we don't care about that." She was intent on seeing to her boy.

"We've got our boy back," Brian added. "That's all that matters to us now."

Undaunted, the man trailed after them and said, "You can still give him what he wanted, you know…what he really wanted for Christmas."

At that, Brian and April stopped short. Frustration and a touch of anger welled up in Brian. He didn't understand the neighbor's interest in something so trivial. April must have felt the same way because she turned on the man as well.

"What are you talking about?" April's voice held an edge.

"In fact," the fuzzy-chinned man said with a sly smile, "you two are the only ones who can truly give him what he really wants." Extending a white-gloved hand, the man gave them a folded slip of paper.

April took the piece of paper, and with Brian looking over her shoulder, she read it in the bright lights of the fire trucks. On the outside, there was one word: *Santa*. She recognized her son's penmanship. On the inside it read:

Dear Santa,
I don't want any toys this year. I have tried real hard to be good, but I must be bad because my mom and dad are so mad all the time. I am sorry. I love them very much. Could you bring them something to make them happy again?
Please.
Sincerely,
Davy

When they glanced up from the letter, the old man was gone. Behind them, Davy stirred and then pulled off the oxygen mask long enough to say, "It was him. It was him, wasn't it?" Then, he fell back again, and a medic put the mask back on his face.

Brian and April looked at one another with wide eyes. Unable to find the words, they hugged one another. They had never felt such joy in their entire lives, and it was enveloped in a new determination to bring genuine happiness into their home. Then, somewhere in the distance they heard the slow, rhythmic tinkle of jingle bells.

MICHAEL DECAMP

Rose and the Wooden Box

"That's a beautiful necklace," the girl said as Rose rang up her purchase. It was a cool April Sunday afternoon in Cutters Notch, Indiana. The trees were beginning to bud, and the little town was as quiet as it could be. There was nothing to see, nothing to do, and no reason for anyone to come into Rose's little convenience store. This girl was only the second customer in the last hour.

"I'm sorry. What was that?" Rose asked as she scanned a package of Twinkies.

"Your necklace," the girl repeated. "It's beautiful. I love that stone. What is it?"

"Oh, this thing?" Rose put her hand up to her neck and touched it. It tingled a little against her fingers. "Actually, I'm not sure what the stone is. I've had it for years. Got it from my grandma when she passed." It was a necessary lie. A tinge of guilt sprang up inside her but then quickly dissipated.

Rose studied the girl making the purchase. She appeared a little older than she first thought. She was, in fact, a grown woman, albeit a young one. Quite pretty—beautiful, actually. The woman had lovely features hinting at genetics from both Africa and somewhere in Asia, maybe Polynesia, maybe Korea. Rose couldn't tell. One thing was clear; she was young. She couldn't be more than maybe twenty with a clear complexion, bright eyes, and an athletic build. The way she carried herself up and down the aisles appeared energetic and smooth. Rose envied her as she watched her shop.

Now in her mid-thirties, Rose began to notice small lines appearing around her eyes and forming at the corners of her mouth when she looked in the mirror. Veins appeared in her legs, and her muscle tone was deteriorating. That dreaded cellulite had begun to form on her thighs. The mirror showed some gray strands of hair alongside her bright red locks too. She was still attractive, despite carrying a few too many pounds. It was getting much more difficult to keep the weight off. Rose could use an injection of youth.

"You don't know what kind of stone it is?" the girl asked with a sad look. "I mean the mixture of colors is sort of strange. At first, I thought it was blue, but on second glance, it appeared more turquoise. Now, it seems kind of green. It's shifting, like one of those old mood rings. I find it almost mesmerizing."

Rose didn't answer right away. Instead, she let her mind take a quick trip. She mentally moved away from the little store with the coolers full of water, sodas, and beer, and the rows of potato chips and candy bars. She traveled back in time to when she first came across the little stone set inside the silver clasp. It had been strung onto the same leather cord that now wrapped around her neck, but that was a long time ago.

She remembered walking up the front steps of the old house. The wooden slats creaked as she crossed to the ornate door made of oak with a giant glass pane in the middle. A knocker hung to one side. She remembered tapping it three times.

"Is it a mood stone of some sort?" the girl broke into her thoughts. "Like it reacts to changes in body heat or something?"

"No, I don't think so," Rose replied. "I'm not sure what it is, but I've never seen another one like it. My grandma said she inherited it from her grandma, who found it out in the woods underneath a large slab of stone." Another lie. Well, much of it, anyway.

"Can I touch it?" The girl reached out her hand.

Rose jerked back and brought her own hand up to block the girl's touch. "No! No, no."

"Hey, I'm sorry," the young woman said. "I'm just a really curious person."

Rose relaxed and leaned back against the wall of cigarettes. *Curiosity can be a dangerous thing.* She took a deep breath and slowly lowered her hand away from the strange necklace that tingled against her fingers.

The girl continued to apologize. "Obviously, I've upset you," she said. "I'm new to town. I'm staying with my friend for a couple of weeks while I'm between jobs. Please forgive me."

"It's okay," Rose said. "I'm just a bit jumpy. Sometimes, I get a little anxious, and when you reached out, it startled me."

"There's no one around. How about I buy you a drink and we can sit and visit for a bit?" the girl suggested. "Maybe I can make it up to you? My name is Sharee. What's yours?"

"Mine is Rose. Nice to meet you. And, you don't need to buy me anything. As an employee, I get all the free coffee I want." Motioning with her left hand, she added, "Have a seat at one of the little tables by the window. I'll be over in a minute."

Rose watched her walk over and sit down. The girl, Sharee, was so smooth and sleek and strong and young. Rose missed that feeling. Lately, aches and pains had shown up in different places along with the age lines and the extra pounds. Getting older was no walk in the park. Being in her thirties was bad enough; she dreaded the forties looming ahead. *What would it be like to go back and be young all over again? Maybe I should let her touch the stone. Maybe for just a few seconds.*

~

Rose was fifteen when she walked up those steps carrying her canvas purse, crossed the wooden porch, and tapped on that ornate oaken door. White sheers covered the inner side of the door's windowpane. Inside, a lamp was lit on a little side table. On the porch where she stood, a swing hung from chains on her right. It was slowly drifting in and out, driven by a slight breeze. To her left, planters of flowers sat on little weatherproof tables. Rose rubbed her hands together—she was late.

~

A couple of hours earlier, she'd been sitting at a

picnic table outside the General, sipping on a bottle of Coke when the little old lady had approached her. Rose didn't see from where she came. The woman just ambled up to the table and sat down with a plop, placing her handbag in front of her—a large white leather bag, almost as big as the woman herself. She placed her bony fingers across the top and stared at Rose.

"Whew," the lady said as she exhaled. "That was a walk. Do you mind if I sit here with you for a bit?" She smiled, revealing a perfect set of white teeth between two lips carefully covered in red lipstick. "These legs ain't what they used to be." Her long silver hair was in a ponytail; she pulled it around, so it rested on her left shoulder.

"Sure. No problem," Rose quipped. It was a lie; actually, she did care. She was waiting on her boyfriend, and she thought the old woman was a little weird. Rose offered a curt smile at her table guest, revealing her own teeth that were a lot less white and in need of braces. "It's a free country. Sit wherever you want."

"You're kind of a sassy one, aren't you? Got some spunk in ya." The old woman continued to smile pleasantly. The sun reflected off her white teeth and sparkled in her blue eyes.

Rose was embarrassed. She didn't really mean to be rude. It was just that the whole situation felt awkward, so she'd blurted out without thinking about how the words sounded. "I'm sorry, ma'am. I didn't mean to be so sassy."

"Don't give it another thought. Let me introduce myself. I'm Minerva Woodstock. I live in the first big house on the left. Up that way," she said and pointed east on 257. "My house sits way back up the long curvy driveway behind the woods, right at the base of the bluff. I've lived there pretty much all my life. I don't come out much, but here I am today."

Ignoring the woman, Rose glanced west, past the traffic light that dangled over Robbins Creek Road and beyond the boarded-up school building. *Where is my boyfriend?* At least, she hoped Roger would be her boyfriend. He was a couple of years older than she and had his own car. Roger was late, though, so she was starting to think he'd stood her up for that Cindy chick again. She grabbed up her soda and took a big swig.

"You seem a little bothered. Have I upset you?" the old woman asked.

"No, no," Rose replied. "Not you. I think my sometimes boyfriend might have skipped on me again."

"Oh, dear, dear," Minerva said. "Men. It seems they just can't help but let their women down. Over the years, I've found them to be so…draining." She smiled. Then, she chuckled, like a joke had just occurred to her.

"Yeah," Rose replied, "it's like they suck the life right out of you."

Minerva continued to smile.

The old woman fiddled in her purse for a few moments, rattling things around. She pulled out an overstuffed wallet, a package of tissues, and a flattened pack of gum before finally yanking a compact mirror from the bottom. Popping it open, she turned around and began to check her makeup in the tiny glass. Rose glanced at her. Their eyes met in the mirror before Minerva returned to the details of her face.

Despite their huge age difference and the fact that Rose was anxious about her boyfriend, the awkwardness of the woman plopping herself down was beginning to wear off. Rose began to find her interesting. She liked the way the woman seemed to have herself put together—stylishly dressed and crisp makeup. Plus, the woman had a sharp tongue. Rose liked that.

After a few moments, Minerva turned back to the table and put everything back into her bag. When she was done, she looked up at Rose. "Listen dear, would you like to make a little money?"

This caught the girl's attention. Cutters Notch wasn't exactly a hotbed of commerce. The only place to get an actual job in town was the General, and she hadn't gotten up the nerve to apply there yet. The only money she had to her name was a five-dollar bill her mom had shoved at her this morning. "Yeah, maybe," Rose answered. Then she added, "How?"

Minerva smiled again, her white teeth reflecting the sun, and distinguished little lines formed around the corners of her eyes. The more Rose saw those impeccable teeth, the more she became self-conscious of her own ragged set.

"Well, my house is quite large," Minerva said, "and I am an old woman, as you can see. I could use some help cleaning up a bit. If you could come over later today and work with me for a couple of hours, I'll give you thirty dollars."

That caught Rose's attention. *Thirty dollars.*

Wow. "I could do that," she said, trying to rein in her enthusiasm. "Seems my boyfriend is ditching me anyway, so I've got nothing else to do."

"Marvelous," Minerva said, her eyes sparkling. "Be at my door in two hours." She glanced at a jewel-encased watch on her left wrist. "It's four o'clock now. I'll see you at six. Okay?"

Rose agreed.

"Keep this little job to yourself, though, dear," Minerva said. "I can't be handing out jobs to all the teenagers around here. Okay?"

Again, Rose agreed. She didn't have many friends anyway.

Without another word, Minerva Woodstock stood up and ambled away. Rose watched her go. Her gait was slow but strong. She moved elegantly along the sidewalk, across the road, and into the driveway that led through the trees to her huge old house. Rose realized that she had never even noticed that driveway before this very moment.

~

The door swung open and Minerva stood smiling in the entryway. "Come on in, dear. Thank you for coming to help an old woman." She pulled the door open, stepped back, and waved her other arm in a welcoming gesture. "Welcome to my humble home."

This house is anything but humble, Rose thought. She'd been amazed at its sheer size as she approached. Balconies with detailed woodwork lined three stories. Turrets rose from the corners with pointed roofs. Trellises flanked the porch with ivy growing all the way to the balcony handrails. Ornate cornices provided decorative trim. The wood siding was painted in varying shades of pastel—pink, yellow, and baby blue were mixed into the different aspects of the architecture in ways that defied explanation but worked amazingly well.

Rose peered around the entryway. To her right was a dining room with giant windows on two walls. The other walls were covered in a wallpaper with a nautical design. A man's portrait hung prominently near the head of an oak table. Antique sconces flanked his bearded face. To her left were a pair of six-panel oak pocket doors. They were closed. She imagined a book-filled library on the other side, maybe with a desk and a couple of reading chairs, too. Straight ahead was a wide, grand, wooden staircase. It led to the center of a landing with a walkway that split off to both the right and the left. The ceiling was three stories up, and a huge chandelier with crystal lights hung from a golden chain into the center of the room.

"Close your mouth, dear," Minerva said. "A fly might buzz in there and get lost."

"This place is amazing," Rose blurted. "I've never been inside a place like this before."

~

"Yes," the old woman replied. "It is, isn't it? My grandfather built it." That was a lie, but a necessary one. "He passed it to my mother, who left it to me." More lies.

~

Suddenly, Rose felt self-conscious. Here she was standing in the richest house that she could imagine, and she was dressed like that pauper from the Dickens novel she'd been forced to read in school the previous month. Her ragged blue jeans sported holes in the knees, her black t-shirt sparkled with sequins on the sleeves, and a pair of red cloth tennis shoes had holes in the toes. Her red hair was pulled back and held with a scrunchie. *At least I have some make up on.*

"Alright, Rose," Minerva said. "I have one particular room I need you to clean for me. It is up those stairs and to the left—the only room down that hallway. You'll find some polish and rags resting on a small table just outside the door. Just go inside and wipe down every surface. Use the polish to bring the wood to a nice shine. Some of the woodwork is too high for me to safely get to these days. If you can do that, you earn the thirty dollars. Does that sound reasonable?"

Thirty dollars. Rose was still amazed she was going to get that much money for helping to clean a little room. Her mom made her clean their small stone house next to the self-service carwash every week, but she still had to beg for every couple of bucks she got. "Yeah, sure. That'll be great."

"Okay, sweetie. Go on up and get started." Minerva gave Rose another smile, again showing her impeccable white teeth. "I'll come up shortly and check on you."

Rose started up the beautiful staircase, but Minerva stopped her at the halfway point. "Oh, by the way, dear. When you go into the room, you'll find a small wooden box on a marble table against the far wall." She paused for a moment like she was remembering something.

"Yes?" Rose prompted her.

"Well, I want you to clean and polish that box, but whatever you do, don't open it." Minerva stared up at Rose with a solemn look on her majestic face. Her high cheekbones were rosy in the light from the chandelier. "Do you understand? You mustn't open it, no matter how curious you become. I can't emphasize enough that you are not to look inside it."

"I understand," Rose said with a nod. "Don't open the box. Got it."

"Excellent. Go on then. I'll see you in a few minutes."

Rose continued up the stairs and turned to the left. "Well, that was creepy," she whispered to herself, "but, whatever. I won't open any stupid wooden box."

~

Rose stood outside the darkly stained, two-panel solid wood door. Everything in the house seemed to be made of hardwood. Her right hand rested on the shiny brass doorknob. There was a small thumb lock above the knob. As Minerva had said, the polish and rags were on a table next to the wall to her right. It was dark where she stood, kind of scary dark.

She turned the knob, let the door swing open, and stepped inside with the cleaning supplies cradled in the crook of her left arm. It was dark inside, too. There was a large window to her left, but with all the shade from the huge trees, little light seeped inside. Feeling around with her free hand, she found a button about where the wall switch should be, so she pushed it. A smaller version of the entryway chandelier and two wall sconces burst to life, blanketing the room in welcome light. Rose's eyes grew wide and her mouth dropped open again.

The small room was shaped like a hexagon. It was one of those turret rooms she had seen as she approached the house. All the walls were covered in dusty amber-colored wood paneling. Cobwebs draped from the light fixtures to the walls to the small marble table against the wall opposite the door. The room looked like no one had been inside for years.

Waving her right arm around, Rose stepped inside and dropped her bag on the floor next to the door. *I don't know if I have enough rags. This is gonna be a chore.* The thirty dollars now seemed a little light.

On the wall above the small marble table with the little wooden box hung another large portrait. This one was of a majestic Native American man. *Weird.* No dust or cobwebs encroached upon the beautiful piece of art. The man in the painting wore a leather shirt with various colorful designs. His hair was long, dark, and interspersed with feathers and beads. His piercing eyes seemed to be staring directly at Rose. She looked away.

The marble table stood about waist high, placing the small wooden box just above her belt. Rose stepped close. The box was made of a darkly stained wood with a flat lid, shaped like the cover of a book. The lid's design was difficult to see through the thick layer of dust, so she bent over for a closer look. Taking one of the rags, she wiped the dust off. It was a symbol of some sort. Rose picked it up to examine the detail. It was a spider in a web. It had fangs and, like the man in the painting, it appeared to be looking directly at her. It was so realistic that she turned the box a little to change the angle. When she did, something rattled and slid against the lowered side. Quickly, she put the box down and jumped back.

"I wonder what that is?" she whispered to herself. Her intense curiosity was attempting to get the best of her again. Her mom often called her a snoop. Once, she'd even secretly opened her Christmas packages at two in the morning and then carefully retaped them so no one would know. Her curiosity was almost an affliction. Still, she'd assured Minerva that she wouldn't open that box, so she shoved the curiosity into her own mental box and set to work on the dust.

A small step stool leaned against the wall, so first she dusted it off. Then, she climbed on top and wiped down the chandelier. She couldn't believe how much dust and cobwebs had collected in the room. *Minerva must never come in here. The dust doesn't look like it's been disturbed in years.* Even as she wiped, her eyes kept glancing back at the box. *What could it hurt to look inside?* She paused. She glanced over her shoulder again. *No.* She forced herself to go back to work. The battle continued between her promise and her curiosity. So far, the promise was winning.

When she finished with the chandelier, she cleaned the wall sconces and then moved on to the window. *There's so much dust in here that it's gonna take me the whole two hours just to dust this room.* Her eyes went back to the container, but she managed to avert them yet again.

"How are you coming along, dear?" Minerva

said from the doorway.

From her position on the step stool where she wiped along the top of the window molding, she glanced back at the old woman who stood just inside the room, smiling up at her with those impeccable teeth. *I wonder how old she actually is.*

"You haven't opened my box, have you?" The old woman's smiling face turned serious.

"No, ma'am," Rose replied.

"Good, good," Minerva said. "Looks like you're doing a good job. I thank you."

"No problem. My momma taught me how to clean and gives me lots of practice."

"Thank you for honoring my request about the box. It contains the key to long life. I've had it for many, many years." The old woman turned and gazed at the box with what seemed to be an air of reverence.

Why does she keep drawing me back to that box? "Really? What is it? Can you at least tell me what's inside?" Rose asked.

"Oh, no, dear," Minerva said. She was still looking at the box, but Rose saw her glance up at her as she spoke. "I'm afraid it's for my eyes and my knowledge only." Then, she suddenly turned her eyes up at Rose and gave her a stern look. "I mean it, girl," her voice gruff. "Do not open that box."

The sudden change of demeanor startled Rose. Up until that moment, the woman had been pleasant, if a little quirky. Now, she seemed downright mean. Minerva's unexpected change hurt Rose. It also angered her. After all, she'd been working so hard at honoring her promise. She stopped her wiping and looked down from the step stool. "I said I wouldn't," she retorted in kind, "and I won't. Okay?"

The woman's gruffness vanished. "I'm sorry, dear," she said. "Sometimes, I get too worked up when I think about the box and the treasure it holds. I'll trust you." As she spoke, she retreated into the hallway. "By the way," she added with a sneer," don't forget to wipe down the backside of the door." Then she reached inside, grabbed the doorknob, and pulled the door closed. She closed it hard. Her muffled laughter echoed down the hallway.

Rose leapt to the floor. Before she could reach the door, the lock engaged from the other side. It was then that it occurred to her that it was strange to have the thumb lock on the outside of the door. Grabbing the knob, she turned it, but the door wouldn't budge. "Hey! Let me out," she screamed. "What are you doing? Let me outta here." There was no answer. The woman's shoes tapped down the hardwood hallway. "Hey, come back here and let me out."

Rose spun, her eyes darting around the room. She ran to the window—huge, heavy, and securely closed. It wouldn't budge. She picked up the step stool made of plastic with aluminum legs that folded on hinges. She tried smashing the window with it, but it wouldn't break. *Plexiglass?* She was stuck. She tried lifting the marble table to throw it against the window, but it was secured to the floor.

She was alone. And, no one knew where she was. She hadn't told anyone, even her mother, that she had this little job. "Let me out," Rose screamed again and again. She shook the door and banged against it. She pounded on the walls. She cried. After a while, she ran out of steam, leaned back against the door, slid down to the floor, and stared across at the little marble table.

Alone with the box.

She wept. She got mad again. After that, she got thirsty. Grabbing her bag, she pulled out a large can of an energy drink, a Red Bull, and she gulped it down. In the end, she got spiteful.

"Screw her," Rose said with a loud voice. "Hey Minerva," she shouted. "So, you don't want me to open the box, huh? Well, screw you, Minerva. I'm in here and you're out there and I'm gonna look in that box."

~

Down the hall, Minerva waited. "I think that ought to about do it." She grinned.

~

Rose stood, picked up the aluminum can and crumbled it, then threw it against the window. Other than a little residual liquid splatter, it left no mark. Then, she marched to the marble table and stood directly in front of it. Staring down at the box, she hesitated. It was like the first time she'd uttered a cuss word, or the first time she'd kissed a boy. Despite her anger, she had to work up the nerve.

There was a little loop and hasp on the front, so she carefully used her right index finger to lift the flat piece of brass free. It stayed up when she released it. Moving the same finger to the right corner of the lid, she tested it. It moved freely. She became so engrossed in opening the box that she didn't hear the large oak door open quietly behind her on well-oiled hinges.

As she slowly lifted the lid, she was half afraid something would jump out at her. But she had to know what was in the stupid box. She lifted it all the way open and then leaned over to look inside. The first thing her eyes landed on was a leather cord. Her gaze followed it until it met a silver setting with a strange stone in the middle. It was the most beautiful stone she'd ever seen. The way the colors shifted was mesmerizing. She couldn't help but pick it up.

There was a mirror on the underside of the box's lid, so she lifted the necklace and held it to her neck. The color of the stone seemed to brighten as it neared her flesh. The color fluctuations held her eyes. Captivating. Hypnotic. She became so entranced that she lost all concept of time and place. She no longer could think of anything but the beautiful, mesmerizing stone.

"Let me tie it in place, dear," Minerva Woodstock said from over Rose's right shoulder.

The woman's bony fingers took the leather cord from her hands. She pulled the stone tightly against Rose's skin. As she watched the necklace attach itself to her neck in the reflection of the mirror, she couldn't recall why she'd been angry with Minerva moments ago. The stone tingled as it touched her. It was like a thousand tiny fingers gripping her skin.

"That's it, Rose. Let's turn you around so I can see how it looks on you." Minerva grasped Rose's shoulders and turned her, so they were face to face.

With her eyes off the stone itself, the spell was broken. Rose remembered what had happened. The old woman had locked her in this room and then laughed about it. Minerva hadn't wanted her to open the box, but now she seemed to be pleased she was wearing the necklace. Rose was confused.

"It won't take long, dear. The stone works quickly."

"What are you talking about?" Rose asked. "What's it doing? It feels weird."

"Why, dear," Minerva seemed pleased and eager to answer. "It's draining your life force, of course." She smiled, again showing those incredibly straight, incredibly white, impeccable teeth. "Once it's finished, I'll remove it."

Rose reached up to pull the stone away, but it was latched on tight. No matter how she scratched at it, she couldn't get it off her neck. It was like a super magnet, sucking the energy out of her. "I can't get it off," she blurted. "It won't come off me!"

"No, it won't come off." Minerva continued to smile and backed off a pace. "Only the owner of the stone can remove it once it's in place. It will only respond to the owner's touch." A note of sadness crossed the woman's face. "I learned that the hard way."

"What are you talking about? Take this off me."

Stepping back again, Minerva leaned against the far wall. "It was 1834 when I first found that necklace in the dirt underneath the edge of a stone slab in the woods. There's a farmhouse near the stone now, but it was all forest then, save our own little cabin. My sister was with me, and she wanted to try it on. I let her. Oh, it was such a sad mistake. I watched the life drain from her face much like I'm watching yours drain now. She scratched and pulled, pulled and scratched, but she couldn't get it off."

Tears escaped the old woman's eyes and drifted down her cheeks.

"I was so sad that I decided to follow her into death. I removed the necklace and put it on myself, but instead of dying as she had, my sister's life force was transferred into my own. I had her thoughts and her memories. I felt her love for me as if it were my own emotion. I'd watched the light drain from her eyes, but then I felt it within myself."

"You're stealing my life?" Rose desperately asked. "This whole thing was just a game to get me to put this on?" Fear mixed with anger inside her.

"Oh, sweetie," Minerva continued. "Yes. Yes, yes. I must do this every twenty to thirty years at a minimum in order to refresh my own life. I cannot do it too often, though. People would begin to ask questions. Once I've infused your life into my own, I'll revert to a much younger version of myself. That younger version will be strong and vibrant. Beautiful again. I might even get your red hair. I hope so. That version of me will become my long-lost daughter or my granddaughter. This version of me will be no more. But, alas, don't worry, dear. Your memories will live on within me."

Terrified, Rose looked desperately at the door and the hallway beyond. *Maybe if I run, if I can get far enough away, I can pull this thing off.*

Minerva watched her eyes. "Go ahead, run. Others have tried. You won't get far. The front door, maybe. Perhaps the driveway. Run. I won't try to stop you." She smiled a sad, knowing smile, but there was a hunger behind it.

With her eyes darting from the door to the old

woman's face, something from her school science class leapt into the front of her mind. *Every animal, when confronted with danger, has two potential reactions*: *Fight or Flight.* Rose made the split decision that if running was useless, then she would give the woman a fight. She'd fight for this life that was her own.

"It's taking a while for the stone to drain you," Minerva observed. "That's unusual. You must have a lot of spunk." She smiled at Rose again. "I like that. I like that a lot."

Rose glanced at the crumpled aluminum can on the floor near the wall. *Ya gotta love caffeine*. Then, she glared at the woman leaning against the wall beside the door. Letting her fear turn fully to rage, Rose let out a scream and rushed at Minerva. "You can't have it," she yelled. "I won't let you have my life. Get this off me now."

~

Minerva Woodstock had drained someone's life force ten, twelve, or maybe fifteen times in the decades that had followed her discovery of the stone and her sister's untimely death. There had been so many years and so many victims that she'd lost count. Each one had tried to run. Always. Every time. Nobody had ever attacked her though. She was completely unprepared for Rose's onslaught.

"Get it off me," Rose screamed as she grabbed the old woman's neck, then tossed Minerva against the doorframe. "Get it off me now!"

For her part, Minerva fell to the floor, then backed away down the hall. If she kept her distance, the stone would do its job. She had to give it time.

~

Rose lowered her head and strode after the woman. The stone was pulling power from her as if she were a draining battery. "You're a freaking little spider, luring me in here. I came to help you, but it was all just an evil trap." She balled up her fists and approached Minerva as the ancient fiend clambered back to her feet near the top of the stairs. "I. Said. Get. This. Off. Of. Me." Each word passing through her clenched teeth.

~

Trying to regain the upper hand, Minerva smiled again. She needed to drain the girl's resolve even as the stone drained her life force. "Now, dear," she said with a syrupy sweetness, "there's no use wasting the short time you have left on bitterness. We all have to go some time; this is your time." Minerva's impeccable teeth were on full display as she projected her confidence.

~

Rose grabbed the woman by the shoulders and lifted her up until they were eye to eye; Minerva's back was to the grand staircase. The chandelier illuminated the cavernous room. Rose glanced over the ancient lady's shoulder and saw that it was a long way down to the bottom.

"How are you doing this?" Minerva asked, genuine fear now showing in her eyes. "You should have been fully drained by now. How?"

Rose, consumed with rage, grinned back Minerva, showing her yellowing, crooked teeth. "You know what they say about Red Bulls. They give you wings." Using what was left of her waning energy, she shoved Minerva backward, down the stairs. "Let's see if you can fly."

Rose slumped as the old woman fell and then cartwheeled down the staircase. She leaned against the handrail, barely holding herself upright, even as Minerva hit the floor, headfirst, at the bottom. Looking down, she could see blood ooze from the ancient hag's lips, and her gray hair splayed out around her. Minerva's head was twisted in an impossible direction, and she wasn't moving.

Collapsing onto the top step, Rose resigned herself to her fate. The "owner" of the necklace was no longer there to remove it. The girl's anger had sealed her own fate. Someone, sometime, would find her in this spot, dead and long gone. Rose closed her eyes and leaned her head against the railing corner post. She was so very tired. Then, she fell back on the floor and closed her eyes.

All at once, energy began to flow in the other direction. It was streaming inside her from the stone, like the tide that ebbed, then changed direction. Like a yard vacuum suddenly becoming a leaf blower. All the power she'd lost was being recharged.

Then, there was more. Rose bolted upright. A visible flow of power left Minerva's body at the foot of the stairs, snaking its way upward like a sliver of mist, and culminating in the stone at her own throat.

Memories began to appear in her mind. Many were Minerva's, and those of others she didn't recognize. Other young girls' faces in the mirror under the box's lid as they tied the stone to their respective throats. She felt their terror. Along with their horror, she also held the memories of their lives that led up to that moment. Their mothers and fathers, brothers and sisters, boyfriends and husbands, even their children. Their lives flashed through Rose's mind like a video being fast-forwarded. She experienced love. She experienced joy. She felt terror and heartbreak. It was nearly overwhelming.

It climaxed as a scene unfolded before her. Rose saw a large stone, flat on top. There were markings there, maybe ancient Native American carvings. She knelt and dug around the base. She felt surprise as her fingers found a leather cord and pulled out the strange necklace from the loose dirt under the edge. "Look what I found," she heard the girl say like it was her own voice. "Isn't it beautiful?"

Another girl was there. She was shorter. It was Minerva's sister; she remembered her as if she were her own. They had shared a room in their family's cabin. They'd eaten eggs and biscuits for breakfast. Their mother had let them go play for a few minutes before they had to start their chores. Rose could feel both love and annoyance toward the little girl. Sometimes, the girl pestered her. Sometimes, they had so much fun together.

"Sure," Minerva said, "Why not?" Rose saw Minerva's hands tie the string around her little sister's neck. Then, she saw the terror in the little girl's eyes, saw her grasp and claw at the stone.

"Get it off!" the girl had shouted. Yet, before she could remove it, the light dimmed and went out of the little girl's eyes. It happened so very fast.

Rose felt Minerva's heart break, felt her guilt. Minerva's hands removed the necklace from her little sister's neck and placed it around her own. She wanted to die, too. It didn't work that way, though. Instead, Minerva felt the power surge inside her, and the little sister's memories became her own. Minerva cried. Now, Rose was crying.

Following the pain of Minerva's personal memories, though, were others that were dark and ominous. Rose didn't recognize the language, but somehow, she understood the words. The images were violent and bloody. Her mind flooded with screams and people running.

Others were struggling against…her…or whoever she had been at that time. She felt human—almost human, anyway. Spears. Arrows. Rocks. Anything that could be flung or swung were being used against the creature she had once been. Strange protuberances stuck out on either side of her face like pincers, and she was hungry, so very hungry.

A brilliant flash of light swept over her and a silver sword swung back and forth, driving her back and back and back. Rose could feel herself being pulled then. It was as if she were being sucked down and down. She screamed. Her hands or paws or claws, whatever they were at the moment, were grasping at the edge of a hole. The necklace had been tied around her right arm. She remembered seeing it there against the strange, dark, hairy skin. The cord came free and as the stone fell off, the memories came to an end.

When the memories stopped flowing, Rose opened her eyes. The stone loosened around her neck, and her face was drenched with sweat.

She looked toward the bottom of the stairs.

Minerva was changing. Her skin wrinkled and dried, and her eyes sank into her skull. Her lips pulled back from her mouth revealing brown, crooked teeth. Her silver-gray hair turned to dust and seemed to evaporate from her head.

Rose stood and slowly crept down the stairs, careful to hold onto the handrail. As she approached the bottom, she turned sideways, keeping her back against the rail, so that she could skirt the quickly disintegrating corpse. Even as she stepped over the old woman, the ancient skin began to follow the hair into oblivion, turning to dust collecting on the hardwood floor.

"Oh, crap," she blurted out. She remembered that her canvas bag was still up in that room with the box. She couldn't leave it there. Leaping over what was left of Minerva, she sprinted back upstairs and grabbed it. Then, as she picked up the empty drink can, she looked over at the still-open box on the marble table.

Rose. It called to her. She heard it in her head. It seemed to be whispering her name. Slowly, she drew near until she could see her reflection. Raising her hand to her neck, the necklace tingled as she touched it. It felt good. So good. She smiled, and in the mirror, she saw her new, beautiful, white, impeccable teeth. They shone bright against her blemish-free, freckled cheeks.

Rose flipped the lid down, grabbed the box, and slipped it into her bag. Then she sprinted down the stairs and leapt over the pile of bones. Stylish clothes that belonged to Minerva Woodstock covered the pile. Quickly, Rose exited the front door.

~

In the convenience store, Rose sat across the small table from Sharee and sipped her coffee. She glanced to her left, only able to make out a remnant of the driveway that led to the old house that used to belong to Minerva Woodstock. It had taken several months before unpaid utility bills and taxes caused authorities to investigate. When they entered and found the bones, they at first assumed foul play, but when tests revealed the remains to be incredibly old, the case was dropped. Where the old woman had gone was a mystery. No one even spoke to Rose about Minerva's disappearance. The house sat empty ever since.

The small wooden box now rested on Rose's nightstand. Each morning, she'd remove the necklace and wear it around. Each night, she placed it back inside. She'd been repeating the process for twenty years.

Rose understood from Minerva's memories that the ideal interval for draining the life force of another and injecting that life force into one's self was ten years. By doing that, the owner of the stone could maintain a consistent age. A longer interval meant a very slow process of aging. To get ahead of the process, the predator could entice victims more often, perhaps every five years. Minerva had allowed herself to grow old gracefully but intended to invite three or four victims at shorter intervals. That pace would dial the clock back by about forty years.

Rose had never entertained the idea of sucking the life out of someone else. Now, however, the effects of aging began to creep into her bones.

Looking at Sharee's clear, smooth skin and athletic form brought a twinge of envy. Two terms from one of the detective novels she liked to read came to mind: motive and opportunity. She had both. She could befriend this girl and lure her to her home. Then, use the stone to transfer Sharee's youthful vigor into her own body. Rose toyed with the idea.

Getting her to try on the necklace would be easy. The girl was already enamored with it. The trick would be disposing of the body.

Rose was daydreaming.

Sharee was chattering, "So, have you lived in this little town all your life?"

"Um, yeah," Rose answered. "I grew up down the road, across from the Notch Inn. My dad used to work in one of the quarries until he was laid off. Then, he went to work for the State Highway Department. Where did you grow up?"

"I'm from Kentucky. Louisville, specifically." Sharee didn't linger on her own history. "What was it like being a teenager in this little town? Was it boring? I can't imagine it. I mean, what did you do for fun?"

I wouldn't have to do anything with the body. There wouldn't be any sign of violence. Sharee would put on the necklace and then collapse. I could just tell the sheriff part of the truth. One minute we were talking...the next minute she fell over. The idea seemed plausible. *Hmm.* "Well, the school was good for activities," Rose answered. "They had the usual. Dances. Football games. Basketball games. When we got old enough to drive, we'd all pile in someone's car and make a run to the Dairy Queen in

Jasper or the Wendy's in French Lick. We found things to do." *Well, that's what the other kids did. I mostly sat at home, alone.*

Sharee rested her elbows on the table and her chin in her hands. Her long curly black hair framed her pretty face. She was smiling at Rose, but her eyes kept drifting back to the stone, sometimes lingering for a few seconds. "I guess it's the same everywhere," Sharee said. "Kids always find stuff to do. I had my church youth group and I played volleyball. Those two things kept me pretty busy."

So, she is an athlete. She probably has good muscle tone. It would be nice to be strong again. Rose lifted her paper coffee cup and took a sip and concentrated on what Sharee was saying.

The conversation continued for a while. Sharee would ask about some aspect of small-town life. Rose would answer the girl's questions as honestly as she could. Then, she would probe a little into Sharee's life. It was like any budding friendship.

All the while, Rose toyed with the envy that had taken root in her mind. She missed being young, sassy, and free to be a little mischievous. On top of that, even when she was young, she never had a complexion as clear and vibrant as Sharee's, at least not until the transfer from Minerva. She wondered what physical features would come to her along with the transfer of Sharee's life force? Minerva's memories told Rose that besides the retraction of biological age, usually some visible physical feature would also cross over. Minerva had hoped to get Rose's red hair.

"We should hang out while I'm in town," Sharee

suddenly said. "My friend has a job over in Paoli. I've got nothing else to do when she's gone. What do you think?"

This was it. Her opening. All she had to do was agree and invite the young beauty over. It would be just that easy. Shivers shot up Rose's spine. She was tingling all over. Adrenaline was making her arms shake a little. *So easy. So very easy. By tomorrow, I could look and feel up to ten years younger.*

"In fact, I've got nothing to do tonight," the young woman added. "What time do you get off work?"

Rose was so nervous and excited that she was having trouble sitting still. She took a deep breath and forced herself to calm down. "I'm off at six."

"Cool. That'll give me some time to call my momma and my granny," Sharee said. "They're back home in Louisville. I'll probably FaceTime them so I can see 'em."

Rose was shaken. She hadn't considered that Sharee had family out there. It hadn't occurred to her that there were people that would be missing the girl.

"My granny is getting pretty old, and she brightens up like a lightning bug when she gets a video call."

Can I do this? Can I really drain someone else's life just to make myself younger? Can I steal this girl from her family? It was as if this aspect of the process had never before crossed her mind. "I don't know if hanging out is a good idea," Rose said. "I'm pretty much a loner, a homebody."

"Are you married?" Sharee replied. "Kids?"

"Well, no. I live alone."

"Then, there's no reason we can't. Let's do it." Sharee's enthusiasm was evident. "Are you game? We'll have something to eat. Maybe watch a movie. It'll be fun."

The girl's eyes sparkled. The curl of Sharee's lips when she smiled created a sense of joy in her heart. She would have fun spending time with her; there was no doubt in her mind about that. *But, can I settle for just that? Can I resist the temptation?*

It had been twenty years since she felt the rush of energy that the stone transferred to her from Minerva. The intensity of the influx of memories was beyond description. It was like she was suddenly a dozen people all at once. While she hadn't done it to anyone else…yet…the memory of that experience was like a piece of peanut butter fudge for a dieter. It tugged and pulled, pulled and tugged. Maybe no one would know. Maybe she could get away with it.

All at once, Rose made her decision. She smacked her palms on the table and gave Sharee a huge grin. "Sure. Let's do it. You can come by my place about seven."

The suddenness of the decision, the smack of the table, and the eagerness in Rose's voice startled Sharee, but she smiled back at her new friend. "Wow," Sharee said. "I like your excitement." Looking at Rose's grin, she paused. "Your teeth are so white and super straight. I guess you must have had braces, huh?"

"Nope," Rose replied. "I inherited these." It wasn't a lie—sort of not, anyway.

"That's amazing. I've never seen anyone with natural teeth that look so impeccable."

"I guess I'm lucky," Rose said softly. "Look, I need to get back to work. I'll see you this evening. I live just east on 257. I'm in the little blue house, this side of the carwash. Okay?"

Sharee agreed, added Rose's number to her contacts, and stood up to leave. "Call me if anything changes, but I'll be there. Thanks."

Rose watched the girl leave, again taken in by the smoothness with which she moved. Sharee almost bounced as she walked. *Oh, to be young again.* She took a deep breath and let out a sigh.

The General was quiet as Rose moved back behind the counter. The coolers buzzed at the other end of the room. She could even hear the hum of the overhead lights. That had been her life for a while—alone. Alone with her thoughts. Alone with her decisions. Alone with her conscience.

She picked up her phone, held the button down, and said, "Call Kevin Flannery." Her brother owned the local hardware store. It was about the only other establishment with a vibrant business in their little town. He sold all sorts of things from bags of potting soil to power tools, handsaws to acidic drain cleaner. He even rented earth-moving equipment.

"Hey, Rose," he said on the other end. "I'm still at the store so I've only got a minute. What's up?"

"I need a couple of things," she answered. "Can you drop them off at my house on your way home?"

"Sure. No problem," he replied. "Whatcha need?"

Rose gave him the list.

~

At 6:30 P.M., Rose stood in her kitchen with

Kevin's material scattered around her. She had Superglue, a shovel, a padlock, a package of large resealable plastic bags, and a medium-size metal toolbox with a padlock hasp installed. Kevin hadn't asked why she wanted this stuff. He'd given up on her quirkiness years before. Instead, he'd gathered the material, added the lock hasp to the toolbox, and dropped the stuff on her back stoop.

Also, on the counter was the old, book-shaped wooden box with the spider image on the top. Slowly, thoughtfully, Rose lifted the lid. So many memories were associated with this box. Most of them did not originate with her. Still, they flooded her mind with a rush of emotion. Tears escaped her eyes and streaked her mascara.

After removing the odd necklace from her neck, she placed it in the box. Then Rose slipped it inside a resealable plastic bag. Finally, she positioned the sealed wooden box inside the metal box. Rose closed the metal lid and flipped the hasp down over the loop. Using the padlock, she locked the necklace inside, but that wasn't enough. She needed it to be even more secure, so she drippled superglue down inside the lock's mechanism.

Rose had made her decision, and she was confident of her choice. Still, she didn't trust herself. So, she was also going to bury the secured package in her backyard and throw the keys into the forest. She would always know the location of the necklace, but she wouldn't be able to easily access it.

Ten minutes later, the chore was complete. The box was buried. The keys were flung. Her hands were washed. Now she sat in her living room and waited for her new friend. Rose smiled, again, her bright white impeccable teeth gleaming. *Youth is fleeting, but friends are even harder to come by.*

MICHAEL DECAMP

Author Bio

Michael DeCamp is the author of both fiction and non-fiction. He is a Christian writer who intersperses faith into his stories in sometimes subtle and sometimes not so subtle ways, but always in a way that will allow anyone to enjoy the stories no matter their personal view of spiritual matters.

A Hoosier native from Muncie, Indiana, his career in industrial sales has allowed him to travel extensively through the rolling hills of southwestern Indiana, providing insight as he builds the weird and often dangerous world of Cutters Notch. He and his wife of over thirty-five years live on the southeast side of Indianapolis. He enjoys cycling, Mexican food, and pushing the boundaries of everyday thought.

Check out his previous works:

Abandon Hope: A Cutters Notch Novel Book 1.

Loving Out Loud: Learning to Love in a Hate-Filled

World.

The sequel to his first Cutters Notch novel, Nozomi's Battle: Book 2 will be out soon. Look for it.

www.ingramcontent.com/pod-product-compliance
Lightning Source LLC
LaVergne TN
LVHW021225080526
838199LV00089B/5833